S0-BZY-821

"I admit it. You're hot." Anna sighed

"But you're not just any hot guy," she continued. "You're the hot guy I work with. I can't sleep with you."

Cole was silent for no more than a second. Then he shrugged. "Okay. I accept that." Without warning, he pulled his thick sweater over his head and tossed it on the bed.

"What do you think you're doing?" Anna asked, her voice cracking.

"Undressing."

"But I thought you were sleeping on the sofa?" Anna meant her voice to sound harsh, but it came out soft.

"No reason we can't sleep in the same room now." Cole cocked an eyebrow at the twin beds.

Anna sat on one and started bouncing.

"What do you think *you're* doing?" Cole repeated her earlier question.

"Testing out which bed is firmer. I love a hard…"

But she had made the mistake of looking at him, and what she'd been about to say died on her lips. He no longer had on his jeans—just a pair of red silk boxer shorts and the biggest…er, smile she'd ever seen.

Dear Reader,

Anybody who's ever made it to adulthood single has probably run into a family member way too interested in their love life. You know the type. Full of questions about why you're not dating, how seriously you are dating or who you should be dating.

In *Cole for Christmas,* Anna Wesley has a houseful of relatives exactly like that. They're so thrilled when she finally brings a man home to dinner that they refuse to believe she and the sexy Cole Mansfield aren't romantically involved.

I hope I've infused this story with the magic of the Christmas season, where love is in the air and anything is possible. Even a sizzling romance between a man who must lie to keep his word and a woman afraid to trust. And, of course, relatives who just might be right about who is Mr. Right.

Happy holidays!

Darlene Gardner

P.S. Online readers can visit me at www.darlenegardner.com.

Books by Darlene Gardner

DARLENE GARDNER

COLE FOR CHRISTMAS

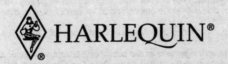

HARLEQUIN®

TORONTO • NEW YORK • LONDON
AMSTERDAM • PARIS • SYDNEY • HAMBURG
STOCKHOLM • ATHENS • TOKYO • MILAN • MADRID
PRAGUE • WARSAW • BUDAPEST • AUCKLAND

If you purchased this book without a cover you should be aware that this book is stolen property. It was reported as "unsold and destroyed" to the publisher, and neither the author nor the publisher has received any payment for this "stripped book."

To my large, loving Polish-American family

ISBN 0-373-69155-6

COLE FOR CHRISTMAS

Copyright © 2003 by Darlene Hrobak Gardner.

All rights reserved. Except for use in any review, the reproduction or utilization of this work in whole or in part in any form by any electronic, mechanical or other means, now known or hereafter invented, including xerography, photocopying and recording, or in any information storage or retrieval system, is forbidden without the written permission of the publisher, Harlequin Enterprises Limited, 225 Duncan Mill Road, Don Mills, Ontario, Canada M3B 3K9.

All characters in this book have no existence outside the imagination of the author and have no relation whatsoever to anyone bearing the same name or names. They are not even distantly inspired by any individual known or unknown to the author, and all incidents are pure invention.

This edition published by arrangement with Harlequin Books S.A.

® and TM are trademarks of the publisher. Trademarks indicated with ® are registered in the United States Patent and Trademark Office, the Canadian Trade Marks Office and in other countries.

Visit us at www.eHarlequin.com

Printed in U.S.A.

1

IF IT WEREN'T FOR Bobblehead Santa, Anna Wesley wouldn't be in this predicament.

She stood next to her desk in the not-quite-deserted marketing offices of Skillington Ski Shops, clutching the eight-inch plastic doll in her right hand, for once not amused by the way its white-haired head danced.

With her left hand, she absently worried the tassel on the Santa Claus hat the family expected her to wear to Christmas Eve dinner that night.

Nobody expected her to bring Bobblehead Santa.

Nobody would know the difference if she'd shown up with a bottle of wine instead of the toy she knew would make her grandfather erupt into one of those belly laughs worthy of St. Nick himself.

But, no, she couldn't do things the easy way. Instead of driving straight to her parents' house, she had to return to the office to pick up the silly doll. An office that should have been empty aside from the once-gay Christmas tree that sat on her secretary's desk, its lights no longer twinkling.

It was nearly seven o'clock. Everybody should have cleared out hours earlier to enjoy what was in Anna's mind the most magical night of the year. Christmas Eve, a night full of anticipation and wonder, meant to be spent in the bosom of family and friends.

That's where she'd be now if she hadn't come back to the office and noticed the light shining under Cole Mansfield's office door.

But maybe she was overreacting. Maybe the cleaning staff had inadvertently left on a light, never mind that it had never happened before.

The shining light didn't necessarily mean her marketing assistant, who'd moved to western Pennsylvania from San Diego to take the job less than a month before, was working late.

She'd no sooner taken a step in the direction of the exit than she heard the whir of a computer printer. Darn. She looked down at Bobblehead Santa, who gazed back up at her with his merry eyes.

"You don't suppose that's the ghost of Christmas Past in there, do you?" she asked him.

He didn't answer but his joy-filled expression remained unchanged. *It's Christmas,* he seemed to say.

"Not everyone celebrates Christmas," she reasoned with him. "He could be Jewish. Or Buddhist. Or Pagan."

Except she remembered the darling red tie he'd been wearing that morning. Festooned with depictions of miniature decorated trees, it played a tinny version of "O, Christmas Tree" whenever he squeezed it.

"That doesn't mean anything. The decorated tree was originally a pagan tradition," she told Bobblehead Santa, but he wasn't buying her excuse.

"All right already, I'll go check on him," she said

grudgingly and headed across the large, airy space to his office.

She paused on the threshold, squaring her shoulders and putting on her title of marketing director of Skillington Ski Shops like a cloak. Then she drew in a deep breath, rapped sharply three times on the door and opened it a crack.

Cole was at his desk, his musical tie loosened, the sleeves of his dress shirt shoved nearly to the elbows of toned arms lightly sprinkled with dark hair. He gave a visible start, then got rid of whatever he'd been staring at on his computer screen.

By the time he turned back to her, he was the picture of innocence, making her think she'd imagined he didn't want her to know what he was working on.

"Hey, boss." He gave her a tired smile. "I didn't think anyone else was still here."

His wavy hair, as black as the image his name conjured, looked as tousled as it did at the end of every day. A faint shadow darkened his chiseled lower jaw. Wire-rimmed glasses dimmed but didn't quite hide the beauty of his deep-blue eyes.

He was sitting down but she already knew he was well over six feet tall and probably topped two hundred pounds. He looked, in short, like a cross between Professor Higgins and the Rock.

Not that she was susceptible to the brainy, testosterone-rich type. Cole had pretty much cured her of that affliction during his job interview when she'd asked his goal and he'd announced that one day he wanted her job.

She hid Bobblehead Santa behind her back and squared her shoulders, summoning the professionalism that was an integral part of her office persona.

"Technically, I'm not still here. I left at noon with everybody else, like I told you to do," she said.

He shrugged. "What can I say? I'm a rebel."

She gave a curt nod and tried not to be threatened by the fact that he was working late.

A less-conscientious supervisor might not have hired Cole, especially because he seemed overqualified for the role of an assistant.

But business at Skillington Ski was stagnant, and Anna couldn't afford to pass over the job candidate most likely to help her market the small chain of ski shops more effectively to western Pennsylvania winter sports enthusiasts.

Besides, she had to admit to a grudging admiration for the way he'd spoken his mind. She'd run into so many liars in her life that she admired people who were forthright about who they were and what they wanted.

Anna wanted to keep her job. Not only was she good at it, she loved it almost as much as the Christmas season.

She didn't intend to let Cole Mansfield have it.

"You're not working late, too, are you?" he asked before she could question him further.

"Not on Christmas Eve," she said, hoping he realized this was the exception rather than the rule. She'd work around the clock to keep her job safe. Then she dredged up the excuse she'd invented in the hall. "I forgot some reports I wanted to look over during the holiday."

Cole leaned back in his chair, a slow smile softening his sculpted features. "Did you remember to hitch your reindeer to a post before you came inside?"

She felt her brow knit, then immediately smoothed it. "Excuse me?" she said in a clipped, no-nonsense voice.

His grin grew wider before he lifted his index finger and pointed to her head, which was covered in...

Oh, no.

With a deft motion, she whipped off the Santa Claus hat and shoved it into the hand holding the bobblehead doll, inadvertently depressing the button at the back of its fur-lined red jacket.

"You sleigh me," the doll said in a squeaky voice.

"Did you say something?" Cole asked, his posture straightening, his dark eyebrows lifting.

"Of course not," she said. Heaven forbid he thought she was flirting with him. Or that he figured out she'd come back to the office for something as ridiculous as Bobblehead Santa. "I didn't hear anything," she fibbed.

"I heard something," he said, then craned his head to the side in an attempt to look around her. "I think it came from behind your back."

"Nonsense." She repositioned herself and squeezed the doll harder to make sure she didn't lose her grip on it.

"Ho, ho, ho," the doll squeaked in its high, cheerful voice.

Cole grinned. "I *know* I heard that."

Resigning herself to defeat, she thrust Bobblehead Santa out in front of her. "I thought my grandfather would get a kick out of him, okay?" she said, annoyed at herself for offering an explanation. She was the boss. She didn't need to explain herself.

"Cute," he said, but he was looking at her rather than the doll.

What was going on? she wondered as her face heated, her stomach lurched and her nerve endings tingled. She seemed to have stepped into an alternate reality where Cole was flirting with her and she was reacting to him. Like a woman reacts to a sexy man.

But that couldn't be. They'd never before been anything other than utterly correct with each other. He lusted after the job she adored. She wasn't attracted to him. She wouldn't let herself be.

"What exactly are you working on?" she asked, bringing the conversation back to a professional level. Where it belonged. "We worked so hard leading up to Christmas that I thought you realized you didn't need to be back in the office until January second."

"I have some ideas for a new brochure rattling around in my head. I figured I should get them down before I lost them."

As if to prove he'd been working, he reached over and pulled a sheet of paper from the printer. When he did so, his back muscles visibly rippled through his dress shirt. Not that she was looking.

No. She was trying to figure out why he'd turned the printout so she couldn't see what was on it. If it had been any other day, Anna would have asked to inspect his work. But she couldn't afford to get absorbed in what he was doing. Not on Christmas Eve.

"This can wait until after the holidays." She made a

mental note to jot down a few ideas of her own in the interim. "I can't give the go-ahead on anything until then."

"I know that, but it's easier to concentrate when the office is empty. Until you came in," he said, giving her a direct look, "there weren't any distractions."

There it was again. The flirting. Again she told herself she had to be mistaken. She'd only imagined the huskiness in his voice. The implied intimacy of the setting, with only the two of them in the office on Christmas Eve, must be affecting her brain. And her palms, which had started to sweat.

Leave, she told herself. *Make like Rudolph and his leggy friends and skedaddle.*

But she couldn't move. Not before she found out what she'd come into his office to learn. She knew she shouldn't ask. She even bit her bottom lip to prevent it, but the question still came tumbling out of her mouth. "Don't you have any plans?"

"Nah," he said.

What did he mean by nah? Everyone who celebrated Christmas and even some of her friends who didn't had holiday plans. Gathering with friends and family was integral to the spirit of the season.

But Cole Mansfield was from California. He'd taken the job at Skillington barely a month ago, a month in which the marketing staff had worked late nearly every night on a sales campaign geared toward Christmas. Cole wouldn't have had time to make friends.

"But surely you must have a family," she said, peering at him intently.

"I'm single," he said, his beautifully shaped dark eyebrows dancing.

"I was referring to your nuclear family," she explained quickly. "You know, brothers and sisters—"

"Don't have any," he interrupted.

"And parents," she continued. "You must have parents."

He laughed, a deep pleasant sound. "I have parents. Two sets of them, in fact."

He didn't offer anything more, which meant, God help her, that she would have to ask. "Didn't either set invite you over for Christmas?"

"Nope."

She tried to keep the shock from her face but was afraid she couldn't quite manage it. He'd proved his arrogance by blithely stating he was gunning for her job, but certainly his parents had managed to overlook that character flaw.

"But surely with four parents..." She paused, trying to think of a tactful way to get her point across. She finally decided there wasn't one. "At least one of them must have wanted you around on Christmas," she finished.

"They would have," he said, "but they're away on vacation."

"Together?" Again she heard the incredulity in her voice.

"Separately." He chuckled. "We're not quite that modern."

Don't do it, her brain screamed. She shouldn't jump to conclusions just because his two sets of parents were off gallivanting somewhere and he was working late on Christmas Eve.

"You weren't planning, by any chance, to spend tonight..." Her voice faltered, and she cleared her throat. *Don't say it*, she thought. "Alone?" she asked.

"Not alone. I'm going to hang with Jimmy Stewart."

Every cell in her body sagged with relief and she sent a silent thank-you to his friend Jimmy.

"I'd be surprised if *It's a Wonderful Life* isn't on TV tonight," he said. "Although I'd rather see Jimmy in *Rear Window* or *Vertigo*."

She nearly groaned aloud. He was referring to Jimmy Stewart, *the actor*. She must have made a pained expression, because he tilted his head quizzically.

"What's the matter. Don't you like Hitchcock?"

"I love him, but even I wouldn't spend Christmas Eve watching his movies," Anna admitted miserably.

"Then what are you doing tonight?"

Walk away, she ordered herself. *Walk away while you still can.*

"I'm having dinner at my parents' house," she answered, then swallowed the huge lump in her throat before she asked the question that had been inevitable since she'd seen the light shining under the door. "Want to come?"

COLE FOLLOWED THE taillights of Anna's Christmas-red Miata through the hilly streets of Shadyside, which looked so different from the flat, palm-tree-dotted southern California landscape that it felt surreal.

But then nothing had been routine for Cole since

seven months ago when he'd inadvertently discovered that the man who raised him wasn't his biological father.

The man who'd helped to give him life had been equally in the dark until Cole had picked up the telephone and called him. After he'd gotten past the initial shock of discovering Cole was his son, they'd instantly hit it off.

Within three months, Cole had a second man in his life he called Dad. Before six months had passed, he'd relocated to the Pittsburgh area in order to fill in the blanks that had always been missing in his life.

That feeling of unreality continued tonight as it sunk in that he was looking forward to the evening ahead.

After scratching plans to fly back to California for the holidays when his parents announced they were taking a Christmas cruise, Cole had originally planned to spend Christmas Eve with his biological father.

It turned out his father's wife had an impromptu vacation to the Hawaiian islands on the mind. Reluctant to leave Cole alone, he'd offered him a plane ticket to Hawaii.

Cole had refused the gift. As much as he burned to get to know his father, he hadn't wanted to be the odd man out at anyone's celebration—until Anna Wesley had walked through his office door wearing her red winter coat and Santa hat.

She'd looked so festive standing there with her cheeks rosy from the cold and her hands clutching the bobblehead doll that going home to an empty apartment had suddenly seemed extremely unappealing.

Anna, surprisingly, had struck him as the picture of appeal.

He followed the Miata through city streets festooned with tiny colorful lights and lampposts hung with Christmas wreaths, refusing to think about the very valid reason he shouldn't fraternize with anyone from work. Especially Anna Wesley.

Surely he wasn't expected to keep the Skillington Ski employees at arm's length on Christmas Eve, he reasoned. Having a holiday dinner with Anna wasn't the same as becoming involved with her. It didn't mean she'd get close enough to him to discover his true motive for taking the job at Skillington.

Eventually they reached a neighborhood of wide, handsome streets and large Victorian homes with candles burning in nearly every window.

After a couple of turns, he followed Anna's example and pulled his SUV up to an already crowded curb next to one of the houses, which was set back on a rectangular lot.

Cole didn't know which was more impressive, the stately beauty of the two-story house or the hundreds of twinkling white lights that turned the place into a winter fantasy land.

He got out of his SUV and joined her on the sidewalk in front of the home, where she seemed to have frozen in place. In addition to the bobblehead doll, she carried a dark-green overnight bag.

She was tall for a woman, probably five eight or nine, with a curvaceous figure and long, shapely legs that were, at the moment, mostly hidden by her calf-length coat.

Her eyes were big and brown, her face heart-shaped and her curly brown hair just long enough to brush her shoulders. She was wearing the Santa hat again but, underneath it, her expression was anything but merry.

"Something wrong?" he prompted, reaching out to touch her on the sleeve of her red coat.

When she stepped away from him and nodded, his stomach pitched to the frozen ground. Could she have guessed his secret? Had he done something tonight to give away that he wasn't exactly what he seemed?

"It struck me while we were driving over here," she said and paused, "that you're a man."

Relief poured through him. She didn't know.

"Last time I checked, that was true. I am a man," he said and wiggled his eyebrows. "You want proof?"

"Of course not," she said in her businesslike office voice, but he thought he caught a fleeting glimpse of something in her doelike eyes. Had it been awareness? "You don't understand. I don't bring men home to my family."

"Ever?" he asked, alarmed that the prospect pleased him.

He'd felt the zing of attraction for her at his job interview, an instantaneous pull that had his loins tightening before she'd said much more than hello.

He'd thought his immediate reaction to her would be a problem, but it had paled over the next month when she'd treated him with an air of detached professionalism.

The coolness was still there, but now the attraction was back. Maybe it had reignited that instant in the office when he'd noticed her brown eyes contained warm golden lights.

"Ever," she confirmed with her customary firmness. "But especially not on holidays. I can't have them jumping to conclusions."

"Aaah," he said as understanding dawned. "You don't want your family to think I'm the boyfriend."

"Exactly." She nodded in the direction of his SUV. "Listen, I'll understand if you make a quick getaway. Unless they're peeking out the windows, nobody's seen you."

She wanted him to nod and go meekly into the night, which would have been the safe choice considering what he was hiding and the way he was reacting to her.

Had they been at work, no doubt she'd have issued an order in that confident way of hers. But they weren't at work and he didn't feel particularly cautious.

"I can handle your family," he said, planting his feet and crossing his arms over his black wool overcoat.

"You don't know my family," she countered, her jaw set at a stubborn angle.

"Then introduce me," he said just as steadfastly.

He would have taken her elbow and steered her toward the door, but she pivoted on her heel and headed for the house without any help from him.

"Fine," she called over her shoulder, "but don't say I didn't warn you."

He followed her up the sidewalk, inexplicably annoyed that she didn't want her family to think of them as a couple.

It didn't seem to matter that up until she'd invited him to dinner, he'd tried very hard not to think of her as anything other than his cool, standoffish boss.

Because now...now his perception of her was changing.

He frowned, uncomfortably aware that he couldn't afford to get too close to her. If he did, he might let it slip that he'd only recently discovered his biological father.

Then her view of him would change, too, only he doubted it would be for the better.

Not when that man was Arthur Skillington, owner and chief executive of the half dozen stores that made up Skillington Ski.

ANNA GAVE HER ELBOW a little shake as she preceded Cole through the door of her parents' house, the better to dislodge his hand, but he held fast.

Didn't the man understand he was adding tinder to a fireplace bound to be blazing without it?

"Let go," she whispered, but evidently not loud enough to supersede the buzz of conversation and the carols that played through the stereo speakers.

"What did you say?"

Cole bent his dark head close, bringing his face so near that she could feel his warm breath on her cheek. Her parents' house smelled of pine needles and pecan pie, but his scent was stronger. Warm wool mixed with something outdoorsy, like the smell of a winter breeze tempered with the heat of his skin.

"I said..." she began and promptly lost her train of thought when he bent closer still. He was so tall that the gesture seemed intimate, as though he couldn't get close enough to her.

Her pulse give a pa-rum-pum-pum-pum worthy of the sticks the little drummer boy pounded in the Christmas carol. Cole grinned, his eyes lighting like the slash of the moon that shined down on the night. Could he have guessed the bizarre effect he had on her?

"Anna, who's that with you?"

It was her mother's voice, so loud and clear it put the silver bells of Christmas to shame.

Anna sprang apart from Cole, feeling the red flame of guilt stain her cheeks. Never mind that she had nothing to feel guilty about.

The foyer opened into a large living area where the family—her parents, aunt and uncle, sister and brother-in-law and grandparents—had congregated beside a tree strung with popcorn, shiny ornaments and colored lights.

Conversation had stopped, leaving only the crackle of the wood in the fireplace and the soft melody of the carols.

"This is Cole Mansfield, Mom. We work together," Anna said, aware that, darn him, he still had hold of her arm. "Cole, this is my mother, Rosemary Wesley."

Her family members emitted a collective hum which, darn them, sounded speculative. Her mother, a small woman with salt-and-pepper hair dressed in a red velour pantsuit, swept to the front of the room where Anna stood with Cole on the hardwood of the entrance-way.

Even though she was married to an obstetrician and lived in a posh part of town, her mother didn't put on airs. She was who she was. A down-to-earth girl from a hardworking Polish family who'd married a prosperous man but had never forgotten her roots.

"My, my, aren't you the hunky one," she said in her too-loud voice as her gaze appreciatively scanned Cole from the thick, black hair on his head to the expensive-looking leather shoes that covered his toes.

Her mother had also never forgotten her family's tendency toward bluntness, Anna mentally added with a silent groan.

"Thank you," Cole said, smiling as though the greeting were perfectly normal.

"I should be thanking you," her mother said, taking both of his hands in hers so that he had to release Anna's elbow. Her mother's eyes danced in her round, friendly face. "You don't know how long we've been waiting for this."

"For what?" Anna asked fearfully.

"You know what." Her mother smiled more brightly than any light in the house. "I had high hopes that you'd finally give in and date Brad Perriman, but this is just as good. Maybe better."

"What's just as good?" Anna asked, not bothering to state that she had zero interest in Brad Perriman. Since her parents had tried to fix her up with him by inviting him to dinner, she'd already said so a half-dozen times.

"Him," her mother said, indicating Cole with the sweep of her hand. "But Anna, you should have told us you were dating someone at work."

"Oh, no." Anna waved her right hand back and forth for emphasis. "We're not dating. I'm Cole's boss." She nudged the solid thickness of Cole's arm with an elbow. "Tell them you work for me, Cole."

"That's true," he said, and Anna could breathe again. "Anna's my boss."

"Well, well, well. Who would have thought Anna would get involved in an office romance." Aunt Miranda, her father's svelte, self-assured sister, came forward on three-inch heels. Her frosted blond hair, combined with winter-white slacks and matching sweater, projected a cool, sophisticated image and made her appear younger than her forty years. "Not that we're not thrilled to finally meet one of her men."

"Anna has a man?" Grandma Ziemanski, who wasn't any taller than Anna's mother and had recently dyed her hair jet black, crossed the room to stand between the other two women and peered up at Cole. "He's kind of big but he's cute. Good going, Anna."

"He's not my man, Grandma," Anna denied sharply.

"If he wasn't your man, you wouldn't have brought him home to meet us," Grandma Ziemanski said brightly, then turned and issued a general invitation. "Hey, everybody, come meet Anna's man."

One by one, like the guests in a receiving line at a wedding, the rest of her family came forward. Her grandfather, uncle and brother-in-law shook Cole's hand, her sister Julie gave him a friendly elbow squeeze and her father slapped him on the back.

If Cole had been her boyfriend, Anna could have tolerated the welcome. Except Cole wasn't her boyfriend. He was the employee with designs on her job.

"Excuse me," Anna said yet again. "Isn't anybody paying attention? Cole and I are *not* dating."

Her father, who was standing closest to them, winked at Cole. He was slender as a reed, with thinning blond hair and an open manner that endeared him to his patients. "That's what she said about Larry Lipinski, and she dated him for six months."

Anna turned to her father in surprise. "You knew I dated Larry?"

"Who's Larry Lipinski?" Cole asked.

Somebody—Anna wasn't sure who, considering most everybody was still congregated at the head of the room—jarred her, causing her to bump into Cole. His arm came around her shoulders, creating such a rush of heat to shoot through her that she was startled into staying where she was.

"Nobody you need worry about, considering that hold you have on my daughter." Her father gave Cole another wink, making Anna wish the pair of them would rise up the chimney, like St. Nick. "She never brought Larry home to meet us."

Considering Larry had lied to her about everything from where he'd gone to college to how many miles he'd logged on his daily run, that wasn't surprising. But she didn't have time to get into that now.

"But—" Anna began again.

"Let me take your coats," her mother said, practically peeling Anna out of hers. Anna felt a little less warm, but not much. Cole shrugged out of his overcoat, revealing his tree-dotted tie. He squeezed it, and a riff from "O, Christmas Tree" sang out.

Grandpa Ziemanski, connoisseur of all things corny, rumbled with laughter. His most prominent feature was his shaven head, but Anna noticed he was the only man in the room that Cole didn't dwarf. Grandpa, however, lacked Cole's muscular build. But not many men who didn't make their living playing professional football were as muscle bound as Cole.

"I like him, Anna," her grandfather said heartily.

"But he's not—"

Grandpa didn't let her finish. "What's that in your hand?" He reached out and took the Bobblehead Santa doll from her, pressing the button at its back.

"Hee, hee, hee," said the Santa doll, his head bobbing crazily. Grandpa mashed the button again, and the doll said, "And I bet you were expecting me to say ho, ho, ho."

Grandpa erupted into more joyous laughter, which was so infectious that Anna couldn't help but chime in. She glanced at Cole to share the moment. Cheerful, masculine rumbles seemed to come from the very center of his being and his blue eyes crinkled behind his professor glasses.

"You've got a great family, Anna," he told her. He reached out and hugged her to him with one long arm, tucking her head under his chin. In light of the laughter and the fact that it was, after all, Christmas Eve, the gesture seemed perfectly natural.

Until her mother called from the entrance to the dining room in her resounding voice.

"Come help Julie and me get out the food, Anna. There'll be enough time for snuggling with your man later."

"We're not snuggling," she denied, shooting out of Cole's embrace so quickly that she stumbled and he had to steady her. She sent him a pleading look and ordered in a low, resolute voice. "Tell them we weren't snuggling."

"I think that was snuggling," Cole said just as quietly.

"Yep," said Grandpa. "That was snuggling, all right."

"Told you," Cole said, his eyes grazing over her as though she were the sexiest woman this side of the North Pole. The room was suddenly so hot Anna felt as though she were standing inches from the fireplace when, in fact, it was fifteen feet away.

"You're not helping," she snapped at Cole.

This was much worse than she'd anticipated. She'd considered the possibility her family might jump to the conclusion that she and Cole were involved, but she hadn't foreseen him acting like he was her boyfriend.

As Anna went to help her mother and sister, she wondered how she could convince her family that nothing was going on between her and Cole.

Especially because she was no longer sure that was true.

2

HIS STOMACH FULL after a traditional meatless dinner of Polish food with strange names like *pierogi* and *kluski*, Cole sat in the glow of a giant Christmas tree watching Anna ignore him.

She stood near a flaming fireplace animatedly talking to her much-rounder, chestnut-haired sister and her boyish brother-in-law, who had apple cheeks and fine, straight hair worn in a bowl cut. She didn't seem to notice that the newlyweds were more engrossed in each other than the conversation.

His eyes drank in the curve of her figure in the red sweater dress she wore, the fall of her curly brown hair, the lovely line of her profile.

She laid a long-fingered, well-shaped hand on her sister's arm, and he couldn't stop from wondering how that hand would feel running over his skin.

Erotic, he thought. Especially if they were both naked.

As though sensing his stare, she looked directly at him. Still imagining her lush body bare, he smiled long and slow.

She didn't return the smile, which was undoubtedly a good thing. If she didn't encourage him, he wouldn't do something stupid: Like make a play for her.

Still, he wanted to believe she kept looking his way because she couldn't help herself. Instead, he had to face the possibility it had something to do with the miniature women perched on either side of him.

"So how long ago did you meet my daughter?" Rosemary Wesley, Anna's mother, sat on the sofa so that her velour-clad body angled toward his. His ears rang. For someone so tiny, she had a monstrous voice box.

"I love how-we-met stories," chimed in Grandma Ziemanski, patting her incongruous black hair into place. He'd already gathered from her own not-nearly-dulcet tones that she was Rosemary's mother. "They're so romantic."

"No romantic story here," Cole said. "I met Anna about a month ago when she interviewed me for the job at Skillington Ski."

He left out the part about the owner of the business being his father, but then he always did. What other choice did he have when Arthur Skillington had asked him to keep their connection on the QT?

"Did she stammer when she asked you questions?" Grandma Ziemanski asked. "That's a dead giveaway that she's nervous."

"Anna would never stammer. That was Julie and she doesn't do it anymore." Rosemary patted Cole on the hand. "So did you know right away you wanted to ask her out?"

Cole thought back to the icy looks that had put his initial attraction to Anna in deep freeze. She'd grilled him relentlessly about why he was pursuing an assistant position when he was qualified to be a marketing director.

He'd claimed to be aiming for her job because he couldn't very well tell her the truth.

The part about him needing work while he was getting to know his father would have been fine. The part about him being a mole trying to figure out why profits were lagging wouldn't have gone over as well.

Cole wanted to reveal his connection to Skillington Ski up front, but Arthur Skillington had talked him out of it. Arthur claimed Cole would be more likely to get to the heart of the problem if the other employees, whose jobs were at risk, weren't on guard around him.

Mostly because he wanted to please a father he'd never known but already loved, Cole had gone along with the plan.

He hadn't let dating Anna enter his mind, primarily because the wrong word from him could get her fired.

"Well, no, I can't say I thought about asking her out right off the bat," he said. "At first, she struck me as...cool."

Grandma Ziemanski's wrinkled hand flew to her chest. "You think Anna's cruel?"

"Not cruel, Mom. Cool. And he doesn't mean now. He meant then." Rosemary leaned across him to get the point across to her mother. "Tell us what you think of Anna now, Cole."

His gaze once again honed in on Anna. Although up to this point her marketing efforts hadn't been enough to pull Skillington Ski out of its slump, at work she struck him as intelligent and competent.

But her mother was interested in his personal assessment. As he tried to form one, firelight danced over her. It infused her golden skin with warmth and made it seem as though her brown hair was spun through with red and gold highlights.

Grandpa Ziemanski snatched the Santa hat from her mop of brown curls and covered his own bald head. When Anna threw back her head and laughed, her face seemed to glow.

"I think she's the most captivating woman I've ever seen," Cole said under his breath.

"Captivating?" Rosemary nodded. "That's a good word. Much less trite than beautiful."

"You don't think Anna's beautiful?" Grandma Ziemanski asked.

Cole jerked his gaze from Anna to her grandmother. "Yes," he refuted quickly. "Yes, of course I think she's beautiful."

"And captivating," Rosemary added, sounding smug. She squeezed his arm. "I knew you felt that way about my daughter the minute I saw you."

"How did you know, Rosie?" Grandma Ziemanski asked.

"The face," Rosemary said. "There's always something glowy around the eyes."

Anna picked that moment to slant him another one of those disapproving looks. A shard of guilt speared through Cole.

She'd spent a good portion of the last few hours trying to make her family understand they weren't dating, and here he was looking at her with "glowy" eyes and expounding on their non-existent romance.

It was a terrible way to repay her for the kindness of asking him to dinner with her warm, wonderful family.

"So when did you change your mind about Anna being cruel and decide you wanted to ask her out?" Grandma Ziemanski asked.

"He didn't say cruel, Mom," Rosemary cut in with an audible tsk. "He said cool."

"Alright already. Then let me put it another way." Grandma Ziemanski peered at him. "When did the cools turn into the hots?"

Cole was about to point out that he didn't have the hots for his boss when he realized he needed to face facts.

A few hours ago, on the sidewalk in front of the house, a definite thaw had begun when he noticed she was nervous about introducing him to her family.

The notion of Anna being apprehensive about anything had thrown him, and he'd glimpsed a different, softer woman in those moments under the starlight.

After watching her talk and laugh with her family over dinner, he'd concluded that woman and not the cool, detached one who came to the office every day was the true Anna.

He tapped his chin with a knuckle while he thought about how to phrase his answer so that it was both truthful and non-inflammatory.

Yes, he was attracted to Anna. But, no, he couldn't become involved with her.

"Anna asked you out first, didn't she?" Rosemary

asked when the moments lengthened without a response. "That's what you don't want to say?"

"No," Cole said quickly, then thought of the invitation to dinner. "I mean yes, but—"

"That Anna has always been too straightforward for her own good," Rosemary said. "Did you know she told Brad Perriman right there in the living room in front of all of us that she didn't want to date him? Not that he accepted that. But in this case, I suppose we should be thankful."

"Look, I should confess something here," Cole began before the women could jump to any more conclusions.

"I already know," Rosemary said. "Don't you think I noticed the way she's been glaring at you?"

"What do you know?" Grandma Ziemanski asked her daughter.

"That Anna made Cole here promise to tell us he was only a friend."

"That's true," Cole said. "But—"

Rosemary patted him on the hand.

"Don't worry about it," she interrupted. "We knew Anna wasn't telling the truth about you not being her boyfriend as soon as we saw you."

WHAT WAS COLE telling her mother and grandmother?

Anna tried to convey with a long, penetrating look that he needed to be careful of what he said.

The main reason she didn't bring home men was that the Ziemanski women seemed to think she needed a husband. Anna wasn't against marriage but she'd yet to have a truly successful relationship.

Before unleashing her family on a man, she needed to be sure she not only loved him but trusted him. The way she'd never trust a man who panted after her job.

She'd had Cole in her sights long enough to notice that teeth were flashing on either side of him. Didn't he realize things weren't going well if her mother and grandmother were smiling?

She'd have to head over there and set things straight but not until Julie and Drew, her sister's husband of three months, understood the situation. She turned back to them.

"So now you see why I couldn't leave Cole all alone in the office on Christmas Eve, right?" she asked.

Julie giggled, prompting Anna to notice that Drew was nuzzling a spot below her sister's ear. She frowned.

"Are you two even listening to me?"

"Listening?" Julie looked at her blankly, then seemed to register what she'd asked. "Oh, yes, listening. Of course we were listening. Weren't we, Drew?"

He peeled his lips off her sister's neck and nodded sheepishly, like she'd caught him with his hand in the cookie jar. "Yes. Cole in the office. You asking him to dinner."

"Only because I felt sorry for him," Anna emphasized. "End of story."

"Would you get me another glass of wine, sweetie?" Julie asked her husband, reaching up on tiptoes to give him a lingering kiss on the mouth.

When he was gone, she rolled her hazel eyes at Anna. "Would you give it up already, Anna? Don't you think we can all tell something's going on between you and Mr. Hunk?''

"My own sister," Anna said through clenched teeth, "and you don't believe me either."

"That's because you've cried wolf once too often."

"If you remember, a wolf does show up in that fairy tale and eats the shepherd boy's sheep," Anna pointed out with heat.

"Wolves don't look at women the way Cole has been looking at you," Julie said, then bit her lip. "Hey, maybe they do." Her face creased into a wide smile. "Lucky you."

How dare he? Anna thought as she mentally reviewed the looks Cole had been giving her. Her sister was right. They did have a wolfish quality.

"Excuse me," she said to Julie and headed straight for Cole.

He was watching her again. Watching her and—she could hardly believe his nerve—smiling.

But not an innocent smile. His teeth weren't visible, his lips had a sensuous curve and his eyes roamed over her with barely concealed appreciation.

Anybody who intercepted that look would probably conclude that he could hardly wait to get her alone, she thought as she stomped toward him.

"Where you going in such a rush?" Her father stepped in front of her so she had to stop or career into him. He was in a conversational group that included her Aunt Miranda and Uncle Peter. "I, for one, would like to hear more about Cole."

"I'm all ears, too," Aunt Miranda said. She slanted a

cool look at her stockbroker husband. "I think we could all take a break from Peter speculating about which stores in the retail sector are providing the best investment opportunities."

"It was more than mere speculation. It was expert analysis," Peter said, stroking his neatly cropped beard and visibly bristling. "Wonder if Cole plays the market."

Cole. If she heard that name one more time, Anna thought she might scream.

"I really wouldn't know," Anna said. "Like I've been telling you, I hardly know him at all."

"Don't you two talk to each other?" her aunt asked before taking a long sip from her glass of white wine.

"Hardly," Anna said. "If you'd been listening to me, you'd know that—"

"I say we get Cole over here so we can all become better acquainted," her father interrupted before beckoning to Cole. "Hey, Cole, the Ziemanski women have had you long enough. Come talk to us Wesleys."

Anna watched as Cole slanted regretful looks at first her mother and then her grandmother, as though he'd actually enjoyed talking to them. He walked up to their group and took a position next to her instead of between her father and uncle, invading her personal space.

She'd never thought of herself as small but her head didn't reach much higher than his extremely broad shoulders. No wonder she imagined she could feel his body heat through the thick jersey knit of her dress.

With his height and muscular build, he had quite a lot of body. She inched away.

"It's Tom, Peter and Miranda, right?" he said to her father, uncle and aunt. They nodded in unison, obviously pleased he remembered their names.

"Anna tells us you two haven't been spending your time together talking," her aunt said, arching a suggestive eyebrow at Cole. Cole, in turn, shot Anna a speculative look.

"I did not say that!" Anna refuted, feeling her face heat.

"It's okay, Anna," her aunt continued. "We're all adults here."

"Must you always say such outrageous things, Miranda?" her husband asked testily. "Anna *is* Tom's daughter."

Her aunt waved a dismissive hand. "Come now, Peter. I'm sure my brother realizes Anna's not an innocent little girl. She is nearly thirty years old."

"I'm twenty-seven," Anna said. "And I didn't—"

"So, Cole," her father interrupted smoothly. "Seems to me I heard your family was from California."

Cole nodded. "San Diego."

"Is it a big family like ours?"

"I'm not as lucky as Anna," Cole said, moving the hand on her back in a caressing motion. Anna would have shifted away if it hadn't felt so good. "Growing up, it was just me and my parents. Their families were spread all over the country so we didn't see them much."

"Then you're an only child?" her father asked.

"I'm my mother's only child." His hand was on her shoulder now, kneading gently. She nearly closed her eyes with pleasure as he rubbed away her tension. "My father has two stepdaughters from his second marriage but I didn't meet them until recently."

"Does your father live in San Diego, too?" Aunt Miranda asked.

He hesitated before answering. "No."

It took Anna a few moments to figure out Cole didn't intend to elaborate. In the month he'd worked at Skillington, Anna hadn't asked him a single personal question. But now a dozen crowded her brain.

"Where does he live?" she pressed.

Again, he took his time answering. "Not far from here."

Interesting, Anna thought. "Is that why you moved to the Pittsburgh area? To be closer to your father?"

"I moved here to take the job at Skillington Ski," he said, which made her remember why she shouldn't let him touch her with such familiarity: he was after her job.

"If your father's in town, why did Anna say you didn't have anywhere else to go tonight?" Uncle Peter asked, frowning.

"My father and his wife are vacationing," Cole said. "My stepsisters live in Texas, and my mother and her husband are in the Bahamas on a cruise."

"So that left you ripe for Anna's picking," Aunt Miranda observed, looking pointedly from one to the other.

"Miranda," Peter said in a warning voice.

"Get with the times, Peter," Aunt Miranda said. "Women pick up men all the time. It's a perfectly acceptable dating practice."

Anna ignored the delicious sensations Cole's gentle massage was causing and figured she'd better distance herself from him, both physically and verbally.

"I didn't pick him up," Anna said, stepping away from him. "I asked him to dinner."

"Am I glad she did." Cole reached over to tuck a strand of hair behind her ear. "I can't think of anyplace I'd rather be."

The tenderness in his touch was reflected on his face, which was quite a feat considering it was made up of hard angles and planes. Not that there wasn't a certain softness around his mouth, which was really quite beautiful when you examined it closely.

The sheer loveliness of that mouth had the power to draw her in. Closer and closer. Until she wondered what it would be like to kiss him.

"What does everybody say to some Christmas carols? Rosemary? You up for some piano playing?" Her grandfather's voice boomed the questions, causing Anna to jerk back.

Her eyes flew to Cole's, which she couldn't read because of the twinkling Christmas tree lights reflected in the lenses of his wire-rimmed glasses.

Had he guessed that she was thinking about kissing him? More to the point, *why* had she been thinking about kissing him? He was hardly her type.

"Oh, no. Not the Christmas carols." Her father let out a melodramatic groan, then whispered to Cole out of the side of his mouth, "My dear wife plays the world's worst piano. And my mother-in-law has a singing voice that could sour wine."

Uncle Peter shuddered. "Never heard anything worse than the two of them together."

"Quick, Cole. Say you'd rather we didn't do the Christmas carols," her father urged. "You're a guest. They might listen to you."

Cole laughed, such a joyous, infectious sound that it seemed to run through Anna's veins along with her blood.

"Not on your life. I might not be much of a singer but I like to sing," Cole said before he walked toward the gleaming mahogany piano at the corner of the room.

Five minutes later, while her mother pounded enthusiastically on the piano keys, Cole led their group in a truly tuneless rendition of "Have Yourself a Merry Little Christmas."

The tassel from the Santa hat he'd plucked from Grandpa's head swung as he swayed to the music, such as it was. A few bars into the song, her mother stopped in midstanza.

"Those are the wrong lyrics," she said crossly and tapped the music on her stand. "Can't you read? I'm playing 'All I Want for Christmas is My Two Front Teeth.'"

A great belly laugh escaped from Grandpa Ziemanski and suddenly Anna couldn't stop herself.

She looked from her indignant mother to her roaring grandfather to a puzzled Cole and burst into laughter. His lips twitched and, after the barest pause, he joined in.

The result was contagious. One by one, everybody in the room began to laugh until there was no sound save the combined chortling of ten people.

Anna's eyes watered and her sides ached. She leaned her head weakly against Cole's chest, thankful when his arms came around her shoulders to support her.

She felt the rumbling inside his chest through her ear and unthinkingly put a hand on his shirt to feel the vibrations.

She could feel the heat coming off his body through his clothes. Experimentally, she moved her hand over the crisp material of his dress shirt. He felt warm and solid, hard muscle covered by smooth flesh. Flesh that no longer vibrated with laughter.

She raised her head to look at him. Her eyes lingered on his mouth, which was no longer laughing, then lifted to his eyes. Even through his glasses, she could see the heat in them.

He was looking at her as though all he wanted for Christmas was *her*.

Sexual awareness shimmied through her, the same way it had in the office when he'd flirted with her. She'd ignored it then, but she couldn't any longer. Not when it was as plain as the Santa hat that covered his lush, dark hair.

Wrenching her gaze from his, she stepped back. He let her go but not so far that she wasn't still in the loose circle of his arms.

"Don't go, sugarplum," he whispered. "You felt good exactly where you were."

She started to pull back despite his words, but her body tingled everywhere it came in contact with his. She hesitated at the same time that her mother crushed the piano keys and the family belted out the lyrics of "Jingle Bells."

She knew she was right about the identity of the song because she glimpsed the music on the piano stand. Cole grinned at her, then sang along in his truly awful baritone.

By the time they were well into another carol, Cole's arms circled her from behind. Before they'd finished for the night, her back was against his chest with his chin resting on the top of her head.

Somehow, she never did muster the will to move.

"I HAD A GREAT TIME," Cole said as Anna's family gathered around him in the foyer. "I can't thank you enough for having me."

Anna's mother handed him the black wool overcoat she took out of the coat closet.

"We're the ones who should thank you for impressing Anna enough that she wanted us to meet you," she said.

Anna didn't rise to that particular bait, possibly because she was occupied with helping him put on his coat. She applied pressure at the small of his back, the better to shove him out the door.

He stubbornly held his ground. He'd bonded with

her family over dinner, caroling and midnight services. He'd be damned if he cut his goodbyes short.

"Me, impress Anna?" he asked rhetorically. He ignored the warning look Anna shot him. "You got that wrong. Anna's the impressive one."

"What a nice thing to say," Grandma Ziemanski offered. "Anna, you better keep this one. When you're as old and set in your ways as you are, there aren't many good ones left."

"Thank you for that thought, Grandma," Anna said wryly. She tapped the face of her watch. "It's late. Cole needs to leave so we can all get to sleep. If we don't, we'll be too tired to enjoy Christmas day."

She pushed at his back but not hard enough to budge him. He didn't spend hours at the gym for nothing.

"Say good-night, Cole," Anna said.

"Good night, everyone," he said, mostly because he couldn't prolong his leave-taking indefinitely. "And Merry Christmas."

"Speaking of Christmas, Cole, what are you doing tomorrow?" Miranda asked. "Peter and I are having everybody over to our house. You're more than welcome to join us."

"Yes," her husband immediately added. "We'd be happy to have you. You and I never did get a chance to talk about the stock market."

Cole's lifting spirits had nothing to do with the Dow Jones Industrial Average. He realized he was reluctant to leave because spending the rest of the holiday alone had lost its appeal.

"He can't come," Anna interjected, shooting him a dagger of a look. "He's busy."

"What could he be busy doing that can't wait until after Christmas?" Rosemary asked incredulously.

Cole kept his mouth shut, especially because Anna's mother had directed the question at her daughter. He crossed his arms over his chest and watched Anna sweat.

"He's busy...working," she said, wiping her brow. Her big, doe eyes flew to him for help, but her mouth flattened when she realized he didn't intend to provide any. "He needs to finish up what he was working on tonight. He can't have any distractions."

Cole sent her a sharp look before it dawned on him that she couldn't possibly know he'd waited until the office was deserted so he could go over the company's marketing plan.

Anna wasn't the retiring type. If she'd guessed what he was doing, she would have said something.

"But it's Christmas," Grandma Ziemanski protested. "Nobody works on Christmas."

"And you're his boss, Anna," Rosemary said. "I know I raised you to be career-minded, but you can't mean to make your boyfriend work on Christmas Day."

"He's not my—" Anna began.

"Of course Cole's not working Christmas Day," her father said. "He's coming to Miranda and Peter's house."

"Maybe he doesn't want to come," Anna said in what was obviously one last-ditch attempt to exclude him from her family's plans.

"Nonsense," Grandpa Ziemanski roared. "The boy wants to spend Christmas with us. Don't you, Cole?"

Cole gazed from the expectant faces of Anna's family members to Anna, who was imperceptibly shaking her head back and forth.

If he did her bidding and said no, he'd risk offending the people who had gone out of their way to make him feel welcome tonight.

Not to mention relegating himself to a lonely Christmas in his new apartment with nothing to keep him company except his miniature Christmas tree, the printouts of Skillington's financial records his father had given him and the memory of the way Anna had felt in his arms.

He gave Anna what he hoped she could tell was an apologetic look before smiling at the people gathered around her.

"Thanks for thinking of me," he said. "I'd love to spend Christmas Day with you."

3

"THIS IS A DISASTER," Anna said after she chased Cole into the cold, calm night. She shivered. She'd been in such a rush to right things that putting on a coat hadn't occurred to her. "What are we going to do now?"

Cole stuck his hands in his pockets, looking maddeningly untroubled by their problem, not to mention impossibly handsome. She bit the inside of her lip. When had she started thinking of him in those terms?

"I thought we'd enjoy each other's company tomorrow," he said.

Anna threw up her hands. "I'd say we did a little too much enjoying tonight. Otherwise we wouldn't be in this predicament."

"I thought tonight went well," he said over his shoulder as he descended the three porch steps to the sidewalk.

The better to make a quick getaway to his car, she thought.

"Tonight did *not* go well," she refuted emphatically as she chased after him. His legs were so much longer than her own long legs that she had to practically run to keep up with him. "You heard my family. They think we're involved."

He was halfway to the car before he abruptly turned

to face her. When he spoke, she could see his breath. "So what? We know we're not so I don't see that it's a problem."

She knew her mouth had dropped open by the cold air that swooshed inside. "How can you say that? Didn't you listen to them tonight? They're probably inside right now talking about what they'll get us for wedding presents."

He laughed and skimmed his fingertips down her cheek. She wasn't sure if her shiver was from his touch or her negligence in putting on a coat to walk him to the car.

"You're exaggerating," he said.

Clouds obscured the moon but the Christmas lights scattered over the property made it possible to read his expression. The harsh lines of his face had softened, and his eyes roamed over her with appreciation. This time her shiver was definitely not from the cold.

"You're doing it again," she accused.

"Doing what?"

She put her hands on her hips. At least she thought they were her hips. She was so frozen she could barely tell where one body part ended and another began. "Touching me. And looking at me like you want to kiss me. No wonder my family thinks we've got something going."

He focused on her lips while his tongue flicked out and licked his bottom one. "I can't help the way I look at you," he said in a hypnotically soft voice.

Her heartbeat sped up but she wasn't about to let him know that. She narrowed her eyes, which had begun to water from the cold. She only hoped her tears didn't ice over. She tried to make her voice harsh. "Sure you can. You don't look at me that way at work."

His eyes roamed over her in the way she was talking about, the way that made her insides melt like chocolate in the sun. "You're different around your family than you are at work," he said. "Softer, more feminine. When I look at you right now, it's easy to forget we work together."

"Then you need to get a better memory, buster, because work is the reason we can't get involved," she said.

She might have sounded more convincing, she thought, if her teeth weren't chattering.

"I agree," he said.

"You do?"

"I do," Cole said so reassuringly that she didn't protest when he took her lightly by the forearms. His hands moved up and down her arms, creating a wonderful friction and chasing away some of the chill. "If you and I get involved, I'd find it too hard to concentrate at work."

"Me, too," she admitted.

At that moment, it was difficult to concentrate on much more than the feel of his hands on her. They were such large, wonderful, *magic* hands. How would they feel, she wondered, on someplace more intimate than her arms? Heavenly, she answered herself.

She cleared her suddenly clogged throat. "Can I ask you something?"

"Um, hmm," he said absently as he continued the delightful massage.

"If we're not getting involved, why are you trying to turn me on?"

"I'm not trying to turn you on." His voice was husky and spiced with deep-toned laughter. "I'm trying to warm you up. It can't be more than thirty degrees out here."

"Oh," Anna said weakly.

"Is it working?"

That depended on whether he was talking about warming her up or turning her on. Hot little pockets of sensation were erupting in places deep inside her but the outer layer of her skin still felt as though she'd been hanging like a slab of beef inside an industrial-sized refrigerator.

"Not entirely," she said.

He let her go, making her fear she'd given the wrong answer. She fisted her hands so she wouldn't reach for him and watched in confusion as he unbuttoned his overcoat. Before she could ask if he was crazy, he drew it open.

"Come here before you freeze to death," he invited.

Said the spider to the fly, she thought. But the promise of warmth plus the chance to be close to him was more temptation than Anna could withstand.

"Oh, all right," she muttered before letting him enfold her in the flaps of his overcoat. Their bodies touched from chest to thigh. Delicious warmth spread through her, and she was honest enough to admit it was only partly due to the coat.

She wrapped her arms around his waist, pressed her cheek to the cool cotton of his shirt and heard his heart rate speed up. Hers was already galloping.

"Nobody better be looking out the window," she murmured without lifting her head. "Otherwise we'll never be able to convince them you're not my boyfriend."

"Does it matter that much what they think?" he asked. His breath was warm against her temple.

"It's not so much what they think as what they'll do," she said. "They're crafty. They like you. They'll throw us together whenever they can."

"Is that why you never brought Larry Lipinski home?"

"I never brought Larry home because he was a chronic liar," she said. "I couldn't trust him."

He was silent for a moment. "Then why did you date him?"

"It's not like I knew he had a Pinocchio complex ahead of time," she said. "But we're getting off the subject. We were talking about why you can't spend tomorrow with us."

She felt his body stiffen. "I already said I would."

"I have an idea about that." She spoke into his chest, finding it easier to deliver her news when she wasn't looking into his devastatingly attractive face. "When I go back inside, I'll tell them you remembered accepting another invitation."

"But I didn't."

"They won't know that. It's the perfect plan."

"You say that like it's already been decided."

Realizing she couldn't drive home her point while talking to his chest, she lifted her head. His sensuously curved lips had thinned and his eyes had hardened into chips of blue ice, not the mark of a happy man.

"It has been decided," she said firmly.

"No," he said, shaking his dark head emphatically. His jaw firmed. "You decided. I didn't. This isn't like at work where your word goes, Anna. Your family invited me. I have some say in whether I show up."

She felt her eyes widen. "You can't mean you actually want to spend Christmas with my family?"

"I like your family," he said. She got ready to argue that he'd never have met her family if it hadn't been for her but he wasn't through talking. "And it would sure beat staying home alone."

The argument died on her lips. Alone, he'd said. "You mean you really don't have plans?"

"I told you. I'm new in town. I don't know many people."

"Nobody invited you over?"

"A couple friends in San Diego, but I decided to stay here. I didn't think it would bother me to spend Christmas alone," he said, then gazed at her so intently she was surprised his glasses didn't fog up. "Until your family invited me to spend it with all of you."

She sighed. "You don't play fair, Cole Mansfield."

A corner of his mouth kicked up. "Does that mean you're as much of a sucker for a guy alone on Christmas Day as you are for one going solo on Christmas Eve?"

"Not quite, but close." Now that they were no longer at odds, she was intensely aware of her body humming in sensual awareness against his. That called to mind, once again, their problem. "Tell you what, you can come tomorrow on one condition."

A fat snowflake drifted down from the sky and hit her nose, distracting her from what she'd been about to say. It was followed by another and then another. She raised her eyes and saw hundreds of white flakes leisurely falling to earth against the gray blanket of night.

"It's snowing," she said, grinning up at him in delight.

Almost instantaneously, she heard voices in the distance break into "I'm Dreaming of a White Christmas." Making sure to stay in the warm circle of Cole's arms, she turned to watch a party breaking up across the street. The departing guests were singing. Most of them had their arms flung around each other.

She giggled. "It looks like the Gumberts can't restrain themselves."

"Neither can I. Not any longer," Cole said in a strangled voice. His arms tightened at her back and she felt the tension in him give way as he gathered her close.

Even before she turned all the way back around, she knew he meant to kiss her. He was so tall that avoiding his mouth would have been a simple matter of bowing her head. Instead, with her blood thrumming and her senses singing, she lifted her head and met him halfway.

In Anna's experience, first kisses were usually clumsy, with neither party sure exactly how to please the other. But Cole's mouth molded to hers as though it had been designed to fit there, like the interlocking piece of a puzzle.

His lips, warm and tasting vaguely of the fine red wine he'd drunk at dinner, moved gently, persuasively against her mouth. The lower part of his face was vaguely scratchy against her smooth skin, underscoring his potent masculinity.

Intoxicating sensations poured through her, surprising in their intensity. She could feel his erection against the lower part of her stomach, and a swirling, liquid heat settled deep inside her.

She moved her hands from his waist, up the hard contours of his chest and circled them around his neck. If she didn't anchor herself, she was afraid she'd get drunk on his kiss and sink bonelessly to the sidewalk.

His tongue slipped inside her mouth, feeling like heated velvet. She moaned, and a heady sensation shot straight to her head.

She *was* getting drunk on his kiss.

She angled her mouth to give him greater access, wanting to get closer to him. She almost cried out in dazed protest when he lifted his head, but then the cool feel of the snow falling on her face penetrated her haze.

The snow reminded her of where she was. She blinked once so that his face came into stark focus. She needed to remind herself of who she was with: Cole Mansfield, the man angling for her job. Lines of strain rimmed his mouth and his glasses were fogged.

"If we don't stop now," he said in a low growl, "I'm afraid your neighbors across the street will get more of a show than they bargained for."

Although an unwise part of her wanted to cling to him, she resolutely loosened her arms from around his neck. She stepped back from the protection of his overcoat and the chill of the night immediately enveloped her.

"So I'll see you tomorrow then," she said, trying to resurrect the businesslike tone she used at the office and failing miserably.

One of his large hands came out to brush the hair back from her face, an intimacy she shouldn't have allowed him. But then hair touching paled in comparison with lip locking. He gave her a sexy, lopsided smile.

"You never did tell me that condition," he said.

She drew a blank until it occurred to her that she had been about to place a provision on him spending Christmas day with her family.

"Of course, the condition," she repeated, stalling while she searched her muddled brain for it. Finally, it came to her. "Tomorrow, you need to make it clear to my family that we're not involved."

His dark eyebrows arched. "In that case, I'll need one to last me."

Before she could guess his intention, he cradled her head between his large hands and brought his mouth down on hers. Their initial kiss had exceeded every expectation she'd ever had about first kisses, but this kiss surpassed it.

This time, there was nothing tentative about the way they came together. Their mouths opened, their tongues tangled in an erotic dance and her insides quaked so hard the rumbling might have registered on the Richter scale.

He held her head steady but it wasn't necessary, not when she couldn't gather the will to move away. Knowing that she shouldn't be kissing him didn't seem to matter, not when the heat was back, making a mockery of the winter night.

She met his passion, ravishing his mouth the same as he did hers. Her mind seemed to switch off so only sensation remained. Again he was the one who drew back, but she couldn't have said for certain how much time had passed: seconds, minutes, hours.

His glasses had fogged again, making it impossible to see his eyes. She had the sensation that he was gazing deeply into hers, looking for some acknowledgment of what they'd just shared that she knew instinctively she shouldn't let him see.

"Good night, sugarplum," he said.

Then he grinned, kissed her on the nose and disappeared down the sidewalk as she stood gazing after him. He whistled a holiday tune that was so off key she couldn't recognize it. She had no trouble identifying the one running through her head, though.

It was "All I Want for Christmas Is You."

COLE WAS HALFWAY OUT the door when the phone rang. He paused, balancing a stack of presents he'd wrapped that morning and a bottle of wine on which he'd placed a merry red bow.

If it had been any other day besides Christmas, he might have let it ring. But he didn't have phone numbers for either set of his parents. If he was going to exchange holiday greetings with family today, this could be his only chance.

He bumped the door closed with his hip, set down his load and picked up the phone on the fourth ring. "Hello."

"Merry Christmas, son."

He smiled, feeling the same connection with Arthur Skillington that had been there from the beginning. Even the phone line didn't dilute it.

"Merry Christmas, Dad," he said, marveling at how easily the salutation came to his lips. Most people went through life with only one father but he'd been blessed with two. "How's the vacation?"

"Hasn't started yet. We've been snowed in since yesterday. Serves me right for booking the Hawaii flight through Detroit. Here's some advice, son. Never change planes in a northern city in the winter."

"That's tough luck," Cole said. "Any chance of getting a flight out later today?"

"Depends on the weather but there's always a chance." His father's gruff voice softened. "Tell you the truth, it hasn't been too bad. They put us up in a fancy hotel and we spent a fortune on room service. Anything's tolerable when you're with the right woman."

That woman being Lilly Skillington, whom he'd married ten years ago well after declaring himself a confirmed bachelor. Cole could easily see how Lilly had changed his father's mind about his marital status. Her features were ordinary and her figure average, but he knew from the enthusiastic way she'd welcomed him into their family that her warm heart was exceptional.

"I'm happy for you and Lilly, Dad. You know that."

"We'd be happier if you were here with us."

"But then I wouldn't get a chance to look over Skillington's financial reports," Cole said. "I got the feeling you were anxious to get my take on them."

"It's nothing that can't wait until after the holidays. I'm more eager for you to enjoy yourself. I don't like you spending Christmas alone."

"I won't be alone," Cole said. "Some...friends invited me over."

"Good, good," Arthur Skillington said, and Cole could hear the relief in his voice. "I was feeling guilty about discouraging you from getting close to the people in the office. I should have realized you'd make other friends."

"Actually," Cole said slowly, "someone from work did invite me over."

"Then I'm glad you refused and accepted the other invitation. Maybe I'm asking too much, but I need you to be completely objective in your assessment of the company."

"You're not asking too much," Cole refuted. For his father, he'd do pretty much anything.

"Good, good." Again Arthur Skillington sounded relieved. "Any ideas yet on what's wrong?"

"It's too soon. I need more time to look at the numbers," Cole said. "But I did want to talk to you about the whole secrecy thing. I'm not sure it's necessary."

"Of course it's necessary. Why do you think I've been

staying away from the office since you started working there? I want a behind-the-scenes look at how the business operates. If everybody knows you're a Skillington, they'll put their best faces forward."

"Maybe some of your employees always do their best, no matter who's around," Cole argued, thinking of Anna.

"Then bully for them. But that remains to be seen, and you're in prime position to see it. We can't change the rules in the middle of the game."

"Maybe the rules aren't fair."

"All's fair in love and business," his father said. "Look, son, I don't want to put you in an awkward position. But this means a lot to me. I'll clean house if that's what it takes to get this business solvent again."

"I want to help you, Dad. You know that," Cole said softly.

"Then let's play it out, see what happens." His father paused. "But forget about that for now. It's Christmas. I want you to enjoy the day."

"I want the same for you," Cole said, but he could only manage to keep half his mind on the rest of the conversation.

The other half was on Anna.

By the time he'd hung up the phone, he'd reached the inescapable conclusion that kissing her had been a mistake.

Not an avoidable mistake, considering how his body had reacted while they were both inside the folds of his overcoat. But still a mistake.

The truth of it was his presence threatened not only

Anna's job security but that of every one of Skillington Ski's employees.

If his father wasn't so adamant about keeping their connection a secret, he'd tell her the truth today. But he couldn't, not with Arthur Skillington counting on him, not when he'd given his word.

He reached once again for the phone, intending to call her aunt's house to send his regrets, but his hand stilled on the receiver.

What would it hurt to spend an innocent day with Anna's family? Yes, he'd enjoyed kissing Anna. But neither of them were comfortable mixing business with pleasure.

Hadn't he and Anna made a pact to demonstrate to her family, and possibly even to themselves, that nothing romantic was between them?

He gathered the presents he'd set on the table, picked up the bottle of wine and walked determinedly to the door.

He was an adult who could not only control his sexual urges but master them. His heartbeat sped up at the memory of how soft and sexy Anna had felt in his arms but he kept walking.

As long as he didn't touch her, he'd be just fine.

"ANNA." HER MOTHER'S VOICE drifted through Aunt Miranda's elegant house to a bright, spacious kitchen where Anna filled silver trays with green spritz cookies shaped like Christmas trees. She'd baked them herself a few days before. "Cole's here."

The cookie in Anna's hand broke clean in two. She

gazed down at it in dismay, then shoved both halves into her mouth. Nobody would accuse her of becoming flustered at Cole's arrival if she could help it.

She was almost finished getting rid of the evidence when it occurred to her that she was alone in the kitchen. Trying desperately to compose herself, she put the tray down and thought about her next move.

Because she wanted to rush to the door, perhaps she should stay in the kitchen. Or maybe it would be best to walk to Cole, very slowly of course, to get the initial greeting over with.

She wasn't aware of deciding on a course of action until she spotted Cole just inside the doorway surrounded by her female relatives. Her mother and grandmother relieved him of a surprising stack of presents while her aunt took his overcoat.

His nose was red from the cold, his hair mussed from the wind and his teeth flashing from the attention.

"You three really know how to make a man feel welcome," he remarked as he brushed snow from his dark hair.

"Men are always welcome here," Aunt Miranda said smoothly.

"Especially if they're with Anna," Grandma Ziemanski added. "We've been worried about her ever finding a man."

Anna would have protested her grandmother's statement if she hadn't been struck speechless by Cole. He towered over the women, a muscular giant wearing a thick red sweater and wire-rimmed glasses that looked delicate when perched on his strong face.

What was happening to her that she thought his professor glasses were sexy? Before she could figure that out, he spotted her.

His smile grew as he gazed at her over the heads of his harem of welcomers. Anna wasn't sure who moved but suddenly she and Cole were close enough that she could feel his breath.

"Merry Christmas, Cole," she said, her voice so breathy she hardly recognized it.

"Merry Christmas, Anna."

Her eyes roamed over his face. Had it really been less than twelve hours since she'd seen him, touched him, kissed him?

Her dreams, she realized, had been full of him. Lovely, hazy dreams in which she felt free to anchor her hands on his shoulders, raise on tiptoe and kiss his descending mouth.

She kissed him now, the way she'd dreamed about. With her fingers spiking through hair slightly damp from melted snow, her mouth open in welcome, her senses swimming in delight.

She closed her eyes, savoring the smell of him, the taste of him, the feel of him.

He smelled of winter, evergreen and the crisp bite of clean air. He tasted of something minty, maybe mouthwash. Even though she'd often thought him too big, at the moment he felt exactly right.

"Mmmmm," she said against his mouth, and felt him smile.

Their lips clung for a few more seconds before he leaned his forehead against hers.

"I like the sound of that mmmmm," he said. "Makes me feel like you won't yell at me for forgetting about our pact."

She groaned but didn't move away, not when she was exactly where she wanted to be. "I forgot about it, too, but maybe we can convince my family we had to kiss because of the mistletoe."

She nodded toward the sprig of leafs and berries hanging from an interior doorway.

"It's twelve feet away," he pointed out, still keeping his hands linked around her waist.

She looked around them. Everybody else had cleared out, leaving them alone in the foyer. "Maybe nobody noticed."

Her sister Julie stuck her head with its riot of reddish-brown curls around the nearest door frame. "Anna, when you and Cole are done kissing, could you help me put out those trays of cookies?"

Julie flashed a welcoming smile at Cole. "Hey, Cole. You can spare her for a few minutes, right? Aunt Miranda likes to have refreshments handy when we're opening presents."

"Sure." Cole loosened his grip on Anna with obvious reluctance. "Unwrapping's hard work. Can't have the family getting hungry."

Julie laughed and closed the space between them until she had Anna by the hand. She tugged.

"Make yourself at home, Cole," Julie called to him as she led Anna toward the kitchen. "You know everybody. Believe me, they'll be welcoming after getting a load of all the presents you brought."

"How could he have had time to buy all those presents?" Anna asked her sister when they were out of Cole's earshot. "He didn't know he was coming with me until last night."

"I don't know the what or the when. All I know is that he came laden with as many gifts as Santa Claus."

"I hope he didn't get me anything," Anna said when she was beside the silver trays of cookies she'd filled earlier.

"Of course he got you something."

"But I don't have anything for him."

Julie actually seemed surprised. "Why not?"

Anna shook her head. Did nobody listen to her? "I'm not going to dignify that with an answer."

"You should have gotten him something," Julie said.

"Ya think?" Anna asked, rubbing her forehead.

"Yeah. I think," Julie said. "Tell you what. I bought Drew a slew of presents. If you want, you can give Cole one of them."

Anna's claim that she and Cole weren't dating might be driven home more successfully if she didn't have a present for him, but she seemed to be in the grip of the giving spirit.

"Really? You'd do that for me?" Anna asked.

"Sure will," Julie said. "I'll just put a new gift tag on one of the presents. Leave it all to me."

COLE RESTED HIS ARM on the back of the oversized love seat, which happened to position said arm directly behind Anna's very nicely shaped shoulders.

She shot him a nervous look. "Remember the pact," she whispered.

"I'm trying, but you could have given a guy a break and laid off the perfume," he said in a quiet voice. "You smell terrific."

An indentation appeared between her eyebrows. "I'm not wearing perfume. Maybe you're smelling my shampoo. It's jasmine-scented."

"Whatever it is, it's driving me crazy," he said as he breathed in her scent. He detected the faint smell of jasmine but something else was mixed with the heady scent. Essence of Anna, he thought.

Her eyes went round. "I'm really driving you crazy?"

She honestly questioned her effect on him, which made it all the more overpowering. "Really," he all but growled.

"Maybe I should move."

"Where to?" he said, gesturing to the crowd in the living room. A member of Anna's family occupied every available sitting area.

"You have a point." She stuck her lower lip out in an adorable pout. "They're here for the duration. They love the opening of the presents."

"Don't start without me," Grandma Ziemanski called, rushing into the room as fast as her short legs would carry her. She surveyed the room, then headed straight for the love seat.

"Move over and I'll squeeze in here," she told her granddaughter.

If Anna hadn't moved flush against him, she would have had an eighty-year-old woman in her lap. The space was so tight that not even a piece of paper could have fit between them, which was fine with Cole.

Anna's body molded against him perfectly, making him supremely glad she wasn't one of those women who was all angles and bones. She felt soft and feminine, from the curve of her hips to the swell of her breasts.

"There's no room, Grandma," he heard Anna tell her grandmother in a small, nervous voice.

"Of course there's room," Grandma Ziemanski refuted. "We're all sitting here, aren't we?"

Cole's muscles strained as he tried to keep his arm from dropping onto Anna's shoulders and pulling her even closer. But then she shifted, bringing her generous right breast more fully against him, and the effort was too much.

His arm dropped and his hand cradled the top of her shoulder. She turned to him, her eyes wide.

"This is not my fault," he whispered, searching her eyes to gauge her mood.

"I know," she said on a sigh.

He felt her relax against him before she gave an audible sniff. "You smell good, too," she said petulantly.

He laughed low in his throat. He'd had a healthy dating life in San Diego and genuinely liked being around women, but he couldn't remember one who appealed to him more than Anna.

It wasn't only the long, leggy look of her that had him enthralled, but her directness. Anna said what she thought. Even if the thought wasn't something he sensed she wanted known.

He was usually forthright as well, but he didn't think it would be wise to say what was on his mind. Not when he wanted to invite her to see whether he felt as good as he smelled.

At the thought of her touching him, his body hardened. She smiled at him, snuggling more fully against him.

"Let's get started," Anna suggested.

Hope flared until, damn it, he realized she was talking about opening the presents.

"Let's," Grandpa Ziemanski said before tearing into a wrapped gift with the vigor of a five-year-old.

Despite the surroundings, it took Cole a full fifteen minutes of watching the unwrapping of everything from a singing plastic trout to an expensive gold watch to get his body under control.

"Let's open the presents from Cole next," Rosemary Wesley suggested as she passed them around to her family members. "Oh, my. There are so many. You didn't have to bring presents for all of us, Cole."

"I wanted to," Cole said. Anna's hair brushed his fingers and he couldn't resist playing with the ends of her dark curls. "You've all been very good to me."

"Of course we've been good to you," Grandma Ziemanski interjected. "Any man of Anna's is a friend of ours."

"But he's not my..." Anna began but didn't finish the sentence. With her side plastered to his and his fingers in her hair, she must have sensed how pointless a denial would be.

"When did you buy all those presents anyway?" Anna asked him as her relatives tore into the gifts.

"I'm in marketing," he whispered back, his mouth brushing the skin along her jaw. He felt a shudder pass through her. Or was that him? "I always have wine and chocolates around. Clients like them."

Her sister Julie held up a box. "Hey, Anna, this one's to you from Cole."

Anna slanted him a suspicious look. "Why do I get the idea that's not chocolate?"

"Because it isn't," he said as Uncle Peter passed the present to her.

She gave him another wary glance, then tore into the package. Not delicately, like most women did, but with a relish that made him wonder if she did everything full steam ahead. Such as making love.

"That looks like a boxed set of movies on DVD," her father said.

"Are they X-rated?" Miranda asked.

"Miranda," Uncle Peter scolded.

"Oh, for goodness' sakes. We're all adults here," Miranda countered. "What kind of movies are they, Anna?"

"Hitchcock movies," Anna said, wonder in her voice.

Her sister Julie clapped. "What a perfect gift. Personally I can't abide suspense movies but Anna adores Hitchcock."

"That's why I gave them to her," Cole said.

"But how did you know I wanted them?" Anna asked.

He could have cleared up the mystery by confiding

he'd treated himself, then decided to give her the movies when she mentioned she liked the director. But he didn't want to. Not when she was looking at him with that soft, awed expression.

He traced the curve of her cheek, enjoying the feel of her smooth skin against the pad of his finger. "I just had the feeling that it would make you happy."

There was a glow about her that wasn't due to the reflection of the Christmas candles burning around the room. He recognized it for what it was: Happiness.

"It did," she said, touching him briefly on the cheek. "Thank you."

"Let's see what Anna got for you, Cole." Miranda rummaged through the presents under the tree. Cole was fairly certain she wouldn't find anything—after all, when had Anna had time to buy him a gift?—when she pulled out a gaily wrapped present.

"Here it is," Miranda said and read from the card, "From Anna to Cole, with all my love."

Cole sent Anna a questioning look and noticed her direct a similar one at her sister. Julie grinned mischievously and shrugged.

It wasn't too difficult to figure out he was about to receive one of the gifts Julie had bought for Drew.

He dutifully unwrapped the present and lifted the lid of a box stamped with the name of a prestigious clothing store.

Reaching inside the box, he moved aside the scarlet-red tissue paper and felt something silky against his fingertips. He clutched the material, pulled it out of the box and held it up to inspect.

''It's a black silk bathrobe,'' Julie said helpfully.

He was about to thank Anna and put the bathrobe back in the package when he noticed something significantly smaller went with it. He dug through the tissue paper until he had hold of it, then pulled it out with a flourish.

It was a very small, very racy black silk thong with a G-string back.

4

AN IMAGE OF COLE wearing the Christmas present and nothing else flashed through Anna's mind.

In the vision, the silky material of the thong couldn't hide his arousal as he sauntered to her on powerfully built legs. One of his eyebrows lifted and there was a sexy tilt to his mouth, which was similar to the way he was looking at her now.

"Why, thank you, Anna." His blue eyes did a devilish dance behind the lenses of his glasses. "I get the feeling this is going to be my best Christmas ever."

The fireplace was clear across the room but suddenly Anna felt as if she were sitting inches away from it. Or maybe even inside it.

He touched his mouth to hers in a kiss that was brief but not innocent. His lips moved over hers suggestively, teasing and tasting and clearly conveying the message that he couldn't wait to get her alone. When he lifted his mouth, his hand lingered on her cheek and his gaze stayed on hers.

"Now that's the kind of gift a woman should give her man," she heard her Aunt Miranda say.

"You gave me cuff links," Uncle Peter pointed out.

"They had diamond studs," her mother interjected. "The women in this family have impeccable taste."

"They're smart, too," Grandma Ziemanski said. "They know that if you want to see a man wearing silk, you have to buy it for him."

"I'd wear silk if you bought it for me," Grandpa Ziemanski said, then paused. "As long as it wasn't red. Or pink. They're not my colors."

"Black was the perfect color choice," Julie said. "Good going, Anna."

Julie's comment snapped Anna out of her kiss-induced stupor. She turned her head, causing Cole's hand to fall from her cheek, and surveyed her relatives.

So much enamel showed that the room could have been the setting for a toothpaste commercial. Even her father and grandfather, the most likely candidates to object to her giving a thong to a man, were smiling.

Nobody except for Julie had the faintest notion the bathrobe and thong had been post-honeymoon gifts from Julie to Drew. Why, Drew was seven or eight inches shorter than Cole. Couldn't her family see the presents wouldn't fit Cole? Especially, she thought as her face colored, the thong?

"Julie." Anna narrowed her eyes to slits as they zeroed in on her sister. "Don't you have something you want to tell everybody?"

"Yes." Julie pressed her hands together and laid her cheek on the bed they made. "I think the two of you make the cutest couple."

Heads bobbed in agreement all over the room, reminding Anna of the confounded Santa Claus bobblehead doll. If she hadn't left that stupid doll in her office on Christmas Eve, she wouldn't be in this mess. But then, a little voice in her head whispered, she wouldn't have known the pleasure of Cole's kiss.

"Thank you," he told her family. "Although I have to say I think Anna's cuter than I am."

His quip made everybody except Anna laugh. She wanted to be angry at him for failing so miserably at convincing her family they weren't involved but she was fair-minded enough to know the failure had been mutual.

In view of the eager way her body responded every time he touched her, maybe it had even been inevitable.

Her grandmother gave her arm a nudge with a bony elbow. "I said it before and I'll say it again. Anna, this one's a keeper."

"I agree," Aunt Miranda said and tapped a long fingernail on a pair of ski goggles that she'd unwrapped a few minutes before. "By the way, that reminds me of something I've been meaning to ask. Anna, you are bringing Cole tomorrow on our—"

Anna couldn't let her finish, not when her aunt was about to bring up the ski vacation Anna was set to take with Miranda, Peter, Julie and Drew. Her parents and grandparents had declined an invitation to accompany them on the basis of severe fear of falling on their butts.

"Let's not talk about tomorrow," Anna said firmly. "Not when we're having such a good time today."

"But—"

"Aren't you the one who always says we should live in the moment, Aunt Miranda? Well, I think this moment is perfect," Anna said. To punctuate her comment, she leaned her head on Cole's substantial shoulder.

"Me, too," Cole said.

His deep voice reverberated through her, eliciting such a pleasant sensation that Anna figured she had inadvertently spoken the truth.

This moment—with the Christmas spirit alive in the air, the fireplace blazing and Cole by her side—really was perfect.

Something magical crackled around her, something that was affecting her senses and making it impossible to resist Cole. But what did she expect? Christmas was a magical time, when fantasy sometimes blurred with reality.

Just because she'd resigned herself to having her family think of Cole as her boyfriend today didn't mean she was locked in to the fiction forever.

She certainly had no intention on taking him along on her much-anticipated ski trip to the charming resort town of White Tower in the hills of northwest Pennsylvania.

When tomorrow came, as it inevitably would, her crazy attraction for Cole would be a thing of the past. Soon afterward, they'd return to being boss and employee.

That was not only the way it had to be, she thought with a stubborn set to her mouth, that was the way it would be.

"YOU DIDN'T HAVE TO drive me home," Anna said as Cole pulled his SUV into a parking space in front of her townhouse and shut off the ignition.

The neighborhood wasn't as grand as the ones in which her parents and aunt and uncle lived but Cole thought it had a certain cozy charm.

Nearly every one of her neighbors had adorned their townhouses with wreaths and tiny colored lights. His favorite decoration, however, was a life-size Santa Claus sitting on a rocking chair with Mrs. Claus in his lap.

"I wanted to drive you home," Cole said. "Besides, I got the impression you didn't have another way back."

"Julie and Drew could have taken me. They live only a few miles from here." She heaved a sigh. "I think they thought we wanted to be alone."

"Then they thought right," Cole said before he opened the door and got out of the car.

Anna didn't strike him as the type who lingered so a man could open her car door but she didn't move from the passenger seat until he came around the SUV. He took her gloveless hand, which felt small and cool in his, and helped her step down from the running board.

"Let's get something straight." She met his gaze straight on, her chin high. "I didn't want to be alone with you."

Because her comment stung, he couldn't resist baiting her. "Afraid you won't be able to resist me?"

"Frankly, yes," she said, then shook her head. "Surely you noticed there's something happening between us." She rolled her eyes. "Believe me, everybody else has."

The snow had stopped hours earlier but not before

coating the entire area with a cool blanket of white. The standing snow combined with the clear, star-sprinkled sky made the night bright enough that he could see her clearly.

She had on the same red coat she'd worn in the office on Christmas Eve but now it was paired with the patterned hat and scarf set in gold, red and blue that were presents from her mother.

With her curly brown hair peeking out from under the hat and spots of red on her cheeks from the cold, she should have looked like the picture of wholesomeness.

So why did she inspire feelings in him that were more naughty than nice?

"I noticed," he said softly, skimming the backs of three fingers across her cheek. "I'm just surprised to hear you admit it."

"Why deny it?" She marched up the winding sidewalk to what he assumed was her townhouse, her booted feet making footprints in the light snow on the sidewalk. As she walked, she talked. "When I have a problem, I like to sink my teeth into it and grind it into submission."

He frowned. That wasn't the sexiest analogy on record but he could go along with it. He'd make it clear he wasn't into biting, but nibbling he didn't mind.

When she unlocked the door, he prepared to follow her inside. But instead of opening it, she leaned her back against it. Her brows were winged, he noticed, making her heart-shaped face look almost elfin. He was instantly enchanted.

"This is what we're going to do," she said, catching her lower lip between her teeth.

His pulse rate sped up. Whatever the plan, he was prepared to agree to it. Even if it did involve minor biting.

"We'll do nothing for a couple of days," she said.

"Do nothing?" he repeated.

"Then I'll tell them we had a fight and broke up."

"Tell who?"

"My family." She scrunched up her forehead. "Who did you think we were talking about?"

He scratched his head. "I thought you were talking about you and me."

"I was," she said. "In relation to my family."

"Then we have another problem."

Her eyebrows rose until they nearly touched the brim of her hat. "We do?"

"Uh-huh." He anchored one hand on the door and leaned closer to her, pinning her between the door and his body. "A big problem. A whopper. You better invite me in so we can hash it out."

She chewed her lower lip and desire shot through him, not entirely unexpected but so powerful that he flinched.

"Why can't we talk about it out here?" she asked.

"Because it's December in Pennsylvania," he said, which wasn't the best reason taking into account that he was overheated despite the chill in the air. He dredged up another one. "And because you have that mulled wine you forgot to take to your aunt's in there."

"I can't imagine you wanting any of that," she said.

"You mean you won't give wine to a thirsty man on Christmas night?" he asked, moving slightly closer to her.

"Well, if you put it that way..." she said, but she sounded wary. As well she should, Cole thought, as he followed her inside the townhouse.

She'd decorated her place in warm shades of gold and green and accented it with various homey touches, such as fresh flowers and a grandfather clock in beautifully aged wood. Cole wouldn't have thought the cozy atmosphere suited Anna just a day before, but he'd learned a lot about her since then.

Anna took off her hat and coat, revealing her gorgeous figure. He forgot all about the décor and shrugged out of his own coat, hoping he'd be staying a while.

"I need a minute to turn on the Christmas lights," Anna said.

He followed her through the townhouse, feeling like she was the Pied Piper and he didn't have any more willpower than a rat. He caught up to her as she was throwing the switch to turn on her Christmas tree lights.

They were red and white, glowing against the green of a tree fragrant with the scent of pine. The combination of colors made him smile, because it was indicative of Anna's personality.

The white lights represented the cool way she dealt with office matters while the red ones depicted the real Anna. The woman who treated her family with warmth and made his blood run hot.

He came up behind her, wrapping his arms around her waist to pull her against him. He heard her draw in a sharp breath and wasn't sure whether it was because he was nuzzling her neck or because she felt him growing hard.

"I thought you wanted some mulled wine," she said. The catch in her voice made his heart skip a beat.

"I don't much like mulled wine," he confessed as he moved her hair out of the way so he could put his lips to her nape. "I never drink it."

"But you said—"

"—Whatever I could think of to get you to invite me in," he finished for her.

"You mean we don't have another problem we need to discuss?"

He flicked out his tongue to tease her neck and felt goose bumps rise on her skin. "Only if you and me being hot for each other is a problem."

She was fighting him and herself. He could feel it in the coiled resistance of her body. He longed to slide his hands up her body and cup her breasts, but he left them at her waist.

"I didn't buy you that black thong," she said.

"I figured that when I noticed the robe was a size medium," he confessed. He rubbed his cheek against her hair. "But that doesn't change the fact that you're still as hot for me as I am for you."

"I wouldn't put it quite that way," she said, but her voice sounded tremulous.

"It's that way." He turned her in his arms so he could see her face, which was flushed and wary. Needing to make her understand, he lifted one of her hands and laid it against the exposed skin of his neck. "See? Can you feel the heat? My whole body's burning for you."

She gulped, and a muscle twitched in her jaw. "That *is* a problem."

"So what do you propose we do about this...heat between us?" he asked softly, searching her face for some sign that she was ready to surrender to the inevitable.

"We've been over this," she said but he was encouraged that she didn't move away. "We can't do anything about it. We work together."

What she said made sense but not for any of the usual reasons. The favor he was doing his father compounded a thousand times the reservations he might normally have about getting romantically involved with his boss.

Hadn't he concluded earlier today that Anna not knowing he was Arthur Skillington's son was a valid reason to keep his hands off her?

He looked down at his hands now, which rested above the curve of her hips, and couldn't make himself let her go. Instead he slid one of those hands up her side and over her rib cage in a long, smooth caress that ended just below the curve of her breast. She made a little sound of pleasure that he silently echoed.

How could something that felt so right be wrong?

Maybe he was thinking about this the wrong way, he reasoned. Maybe a relationship between them wasn't such a bad idea after all.

He hadn't exactly lied to her. Even though he was linked by blood to Arthur Skillington, his last name was

Mansfield and always had been. And what purer motives could a son have than a willingness to help his father in a time of need?

Surely when the time came Anna would understand why he hadn't been at liberty to tell her Arthur Skillington was his biological father.

"I'm very good at keeping my business life separate from my private life," Cole said.

He was, too. He felt sure he could provide Arthur Skillington with his unbiased opinion about why profits were stagnating. No matter what happened between Anna and him.

"What if I'm not?" she asked.

Her lips were slightly parted and so tempting he couldn't resist running his fingertips over them.

"Then I'll be the strong one. If you get the urge to kiss me in the office, I'll pull you into a closet."

"Be serious," she said, but she giggled.

His restless hands ran down her arms and back up, pausing just shy of the swell of her breasts. "Don't you want to be inside a closet with me?"

"It's unprofessional," she hedged.

"Then I'll have to think of something else."

"Like what?" she asked, her breath playing lightly over his face.

He pulled her flush against him, lowered his head and nuzzled her temple. "I'll write you naughty e-mails until we're both panting from them. Then, as soon as we're both off the clock, I'll get you in a compromising situation."

"You mean, like this?"

He rubbed his lower body against hers, enjoying the friction. "Exactly like this."

She gazed up at him. Her eyes caught the sheen from the Christmas tree lights and glowed red. "Would you kiss me?"

"Oh, yeah," he said and did exactly that.

He'd meant to kiss her like he had before, with slow deliberation so she could get used to the liberty he was taking. But at the first taste of her, he lost sight of his plan. He coaxed her lips apart and boldly stroked her tongue with his, instantly growing so hard that he hurt.

She wrapped her arms around his neck and pressed herself against him, kissing him back until he was dizzy with wanting her. She was perfect, he thought dimly. An ice queen at the office, full of warmth with her family, flames in his arms.

She was even the right height, not so small that she had to stand on tiptoe to kiss him but tall enough that she wasn't choking him as she brought his head down to hers.

He cupped her lush bottom with one hand, squeezing gently. Then his hands glided up her body, trailing over her flat stomach to linger at the generous mounds of her breasts.

He thrust his tongue deeper into her mouth at the same time he caressed her breasts. His hand met with a frustrating barrier of material. He'd thought her green sweater decorated with snowmen and reindeer cute before, but now he wanted it out of the way.

Impatiently he shoved the sweater up her body and reached under it. His reward was the smooth skin of her stomach. He let his hand drift higher still until it slipped inside her bra. Groaning, he kneaded the soft flesh.

"Cole," she said against his mouth. "Feels... so...good."

In a flash, he pulled her sweater over her head. Her bra was black lace, yet another surprise. He would have guessed the Anna of the office wore simple white undergarments. He preferred this variety but would like it better when it was no longer in his way. The bra unfastened in the front, which should have made it easier to remove, but his hands were so unsteady it took him three tries to get it off.

Then she was naked from the waist up and so beautiful his throat thickened. Her breasts were a few shades lighter than the rest of her, telling him she spent a lot of the summer outdoors. Her nipple area was a soft brown, like her hair. He lowered his mouth, wanting to taste her, and she fisted her hands in his hair as he laved her breast.

Then they were sinking until they were on their knees in front of the Christmas tree. Had he pulled her down or had she yanked him? Or had their legs suddenly gone so weak they couldn't provide support?

He dove in for another go at her mouth, which was already red and moist from his kisses. His chest heaved when he drew back for a breath. Because he couldn't stop touching her, not even for a moment, he cupped her cheek. She gazed at him, her eyes bright with passion and...distrust?

He sighed. Before they proceeded any further, he

needed to make her understand. "I want you, Anna. And, believe me, it has nothing to do with us working together."

When she wrenched away from him, he was so surprised he let her go. He watched with puzzlement and frustration as she cast around on the floor for her sweater. Her hands shook, betraying that she'd been as turned on as he still was.

"Anna?" he asked questioningly, sounding a little desperate even to his own ears. "What's going on?"

"You reminded me of why we can't do this," she said, her voice shaky.

"I didn't mean to." He rubbed his brow in frustration and adjusted his glasses, which were slightly askew. "Wait a minute, why can't we do this?"

"Because of work." She pulled the sweater over her head, covering her gorgeous breasts. "Because you want my job."

"What I want is you," he whispered. He moved until he was close enough to put a hand over her heart. It thundered in time to the beat of his. "You want me, too."

She closed her eyes, but he'd read the truth before the shutter of her eyelids hid it. He wasn't wrong. She did want him.

He waited, hoping she'd lose the struggle she seemed to be waging against herself. After a moment, she opened her eyes. He could see the white and red lights of the Christmas tree reflected in her brown irises.

"When I was a little girl, I used to make a Christmas wish list for Santa," she said softly, as though telling him something vitally important. "Every year, at the very top of the list, I'd put a potbellied pig."

He typically would have enjoyed listening to a story about her childhood, but this wasn't one of those times. He sat back on the floor and forced himself to ask, "Why a pig?"

"Not just any pig," she corrected. "A potbellied pig. One of them followed me around once at a petting zoo. I fell in love with his pink nose and fat little belly. From that moment on, I wanted a potbellied pig more than anything in the world."

He was silent, waiting for her to continue, wondering what relevance her story had to what was happening between them.

"So every year on Christmas, I'd get up before dawn and rush downstairs. I was sure the pig would be waiting for me under the tree with a big red ribbon tied around its thick neck."

"Let me guess? It never was."

She swallowed and shook her head. When she spoke, her voice cracked. "No matter how many presents I got, I was always a little sad because I didn't get that pig."

The corners of her mouth turned downward. "My parents would say Santa knew best, that it wasn't fair to keep an animal cooped up in the house for half the year, that we weren't the kind of people who could potty-train a pig.

"And of course they were right. But I wanted that potbellied pig so badly I ached for it. It was only when I got older that I learned the lesson that's stuck with me all these years."

"What lesson is that?" he asked in a low voice.

"Not only can't you always get what you want, but it's not smart to want what you shouldn't have."

He was silent for long moments while he thought about what she'd said. The only sounds in the house were the quiet whir of her heater and their soft breaths but he felt like shouting at the unfairness of it all. Instead, he said, "I gather you're putting me and the pot-bellied pig in the same category."

"Exactly," Anna said with a nod. She sounded as though she were relieved he understood. But he didn't understand at all.

"You can't stop yourself from wanting," he argued.

"Maybe so. But I can stop myself from taking what I want." She cleared her throat and rose to her feet, bending down to smooth her pant legs. "Now that we've got that straight, I think it's best if you leave."

He didn't want to go, not when he could make her forget she shouldn't want him simply by kissing her again.

But he couldn't do that. Anna wasn't yet ready to acknowledge that what was growing between them was as inevitable as the dawn.

"I think it's best if I go, too," he said and got up from the floor.

"You do?" She seemed oddly insulted, giving fuel to the plan brewing in his head. "I mean of course you do."

A few minutes later, when he was outside in the cold on her small porch, she hesitated at her open door for a tell-tale instant.

"Well, then." She attempted a smile that fell shy of the mark. "Merry Christmas, Cole."

"Merry Christmas, Anna."

"I guess I'll see you at work then."

She stared at him, her eyes soft and intent as though she didn't want to say goodbye.

"Yes, you will," he said, and she nodded once before closing the door with a soft thud. He could have told her she'd see him well before then, but he wanted to surprise her.

She couldn't have a potbellied pig for Christmas, but he intended to make her realize she could have him.

5

ANNA'S STOCKINGED TOES sunk in the plush champagne-colored carpeting as she crossed the great room of the chalet. Her legs were pleasantly tired from a day of skiing.

She plopped down on the overstuffed sofa next to her aunt and gazed toward one of the large front windows. White flakes fell against the dark-gray blanket of night, fluttering softly to an earth already packed with six inches of snow.

"It's starting to really come down out there," she remarked to Miranda. "Good thing we rented a place within walking distance of the lodge. Otherwise, we might not get any dinner tonight."

She put emphasis on the word *dinner*, which caused her mouth to water.

"After all that skiing," she added, "I sure am hungry."

Aunt Miranda didn't glance up from her fashion magazine. Uncle Peter, who'd cried off skiing because he said he had work to do, was in the same position as he'd been when they returned from the slopes: hunched over his laptop computer at a corner desk. Julie and Drew sat closely together in front of the crackling fireplace, whispering to each other amidst kisses and giggles.

Anna's stomach gave a noisy rumble but nobody paid it—or her—any attention.

"Hello, people. I'm talking over here," Anna said, waving her arms. After a few seconds, everybody except Uncle Peter looked up. "That was a thinly veiled suggestion that we go to dinner."

Julie's freckled face took on a curiously reluctant expression. "I don't think we should go just yet."

"Why not? Skiing burns up the calories and we were at it all day." Anna picked up one of the shiny plastic apples in the basket of fake fruit on the table. "If we don't eat soon, I'll be forced to try my luck with this."

"My brother bit into a bogus pear once when we were kids, and he broke his front tooth," Drew said. "The dentist gave him hell."

"My dentist's a skier," Anna said. "He'd understand."

Julie unglued herself from Drew's side and casually walked to one of the chalet's front windows, which overlooked the curving one-lane road that snaked up the mountain. She craned her head, as though looking for something.

"I still think we should wait," Julie said.

"If we wait much longer, the snow will be too deep to trudge through," Anna said. "And why do you keep looking out the window?"

Julie gave a guilty start. "I don't keep looking out the window," she said.

"You're a rotten liar, Julie," Aunt Miranda said.

"Your sister's smart enough to figure out that something's up."

For one of the few times since they'd come back to the chalet, Uncle Peter gave something besides the computer his attention. "So of course you have to blurt out what it is and ruin everything."

"I'm not ruining anything," Aunt Miranda said crisply. "I'm merely pointing out that Anna must know she's in for a surprise."

"What kind of surprise?" Anna asked suspiciously.

Julie clapped her hands at the same time Anna noticed the glow of headlights turning into the chalet's driveway. Her sister whirled around, a gigantic smile wreathing her face.

"A wonderful surprise," she told Anna before she rushed across the room, grabbed her by the hand and pulled her off the sofa. "You're going to love it."

Alarm skittered through Anna, which she tried to rationalize away. Even though subconsciously she'd been waiting all day for something like this, Julie's surprise didn't necessarily have to be a person.

Whoever had pulled into the driveway could be delivering something, like pizza or a new pair of ski goggles. She could use those. One of the eyepieces on hers had a scratch down the center.

Julie, who had a firm hold on her hand, closed in fast on the front door. Her sister had been acting strangely, certainly, but that didn't necessarily mean she'd overstepped her bounds and invited...

"Cole," Julie exclaimed when she yanked open the

front door. "Are we glad you're here. Anna couldn't wait any longer."

He came into the house with snowflakes dusting his dark hair, his skin ruddy from the cold, his teeth visible in a smile that seemed to be for Anna alone.

Heat slashed through her and zoomed southward.

"Is that right?" he asked, bending down from his lofty height to kiss Julie's cheek in a brief hello. "And here I thought I was a Christmas surprise."

"You're a surprise all right," Anna said dryly. She tried to make her eyes flash displeasure instead of the lust that had been churning inside her since their aborted lovemaking session the night before.

She briefly considered telling her family all over again that she and Cole weren't dating, but figured the denial wouldn't hold much credence with him standing in their vacation home. That didn't mean she had to be spineless.

"Julie didn't mean I couldn't wait for you. She meant I can't wait any longer for dinner."

He dropped his bag onto the hardwood of the foyer, raised his eyebrows and sauntered up to her. Wearing his overcoat, he was a formidable sight. Six feet four of burly, sexy male.

"What if you have dessert first?" he asked before he lowered his head.

His lips were cool but moved over hers with a fiery possessiveness that made it clear to anybody watching that they were a couple.

But darn it, Anna thought even as her lips clung to his, they weren't even dating. She'd made that crystal-clear to him less than twenty-four hours ago. He worked for her, for goodness' sake. Even as her toes curled inside the thick wool of her socks, she felt her temper rising.

"Glad to see me?" he asked when he drew back. The steam their kiss had generated coated his glasses so she couldn't see his eyes, but she sensed they were sparkling.

"No," she said in a low, furious voice. "I am not glad to see you."

"Liar," he whispered before dropping a kiss on her nose and heading toward the great room.

"Hey, Miranda, Peter, Drew," he said, smiling at everyone in turn. "Good to see you all again."

"How are the roads?" Drew asked.

"Bad and getting worse," Cole answered.

Peter lifted his head from the computer screen and rested his hands on the edge of the desk. "We were worried you might not make it up here tonight."

"Did everybody know he was coming except for me?" Anna asked in exasperation.

"Yes," Julie said while taking Cole's coat. "We all thought it would be a wonderful Christmas surprise."

"Imagine that," she murmured while she tried to get her infernal heartbeat to slow.

"I talked Cole into coming," Julie said proudly. "I know you said he needed to work, Anna, but I persuaded him to bring his work along like Uncle Peter did."

"Hopefully for your sake, Anna, Cole's not like Peter," Aunt Miranda said. "Show him how comfortable the bedrooms are. Surely that will convince him there are better things to do with his time than work."

"Miranda," Peter said in his typical warning tone while Anna felt her face color. She usually enjoyed her aunt's candid comments, but most of the time they weren't directed at her.

"You'll be sharing a room with Anna, of course," Julie said. "The chalet only has the three bedrooms."

At the announcement, Cole sent Anna an apologetic look and shrugged his impossibly broad shoulders, as though he hadn't foreseen the development. *Yeah, right,* she thought.

"If Anna would rather, I'll sleep on the sofa," he offered.

Aunt Miranda let out a trill of laughter so boisterous she nearly doubled over from it.

"I don't think," she said between chortles, "that my niece is stupid enough to let a man like you sleep on the sofa."

"Of course I won't make Cole sleep on the sofa," Anna said, ignoring the way her heart hammered at the surprised, anticipatory look that passed Cole's handsome features. He probably envisioned a cozy little room with a big, inviting bed. "The twin beds in my room are perfectly comfortable."

The hope disappeared from his expression, but Anna refused to categorize the hollow feeling that overtook her as disappointment.

Even if it was.

COLE SIDESTEPPED the spray of snow that Anna's booted feet kicked up, hoping she hadn't misfired while intending him to be the target.

He was a smart guy. He'd interpreted all those annoyed looks Anna had slanted him during dinner at the lodge as warning signals. Well before he'd taken his last bite of prime rib, he figured the walk back to the chalet would be hazardous for more reasons than slippery patches of ice.

He and Anna hadn't been without his safety net—Miranda, Peter, Julie and Drew—since he'd sprung his surprise visit on her. As Anna gave the snow another kick, he figured that was a good thing.

"You're being awfully hard on that snow, Anna," Julie said from the circle of Drew's arm.

"Maybe I'm miffed because it won't stop falling."

"That's funny," Julie said. "Ever since we were kids, you always liked the white stuff."

"I still do," Anna said. "But it's snowing so hard, it'll be impossible for anybody to drive back down the mountain tonight."

She glared pointedly at Cole, and he frowned. When he'd accepted Julie's offer to join them on their ski vacation, he guessed Anna would be resistant. But deep down he believed she wanted him along as much as he wanted to be there. What if that weren't true?

He struggled with himself for a moment before reluctantly concluding there was only one gentlemanly thing to do. "I could probably get down the hill if I tried."

"It's not a hill, it's a mountain," Julie said. "And nobody wants you to drive down it. Especially not Anna."

Aunt Miranda turned her neck around so far, she resembled Linda Blair in *The Exorcist*. "Am I missing something? Are Cole and Anna having a fight?"

"No, we are not having a fight," Anna said, but it still seemed to Cole that she wanted to slug him.

"Then why do you want him to drive down the mountain tonight in hazardous conditions?"

"I don't want him to," Anna snapped.

"See, Cole," Julie said. "I told you she liked having you around."

"I wish I didn't," she muttered so softly that no one other than Cole could hear.

Anna gave the snow yet another kick, a harder one this time. Her anchor leg slipped on an icy patch and she lost her balance.

Cole reached for her at the same time her body slammed into him, barely managing to keep his feet as he steadied her. She gazed up at him, a stunned look on a face he found more compelling by the minute. Snow fell on her golden skin, evaporating as soon as it hit, leaving her with a dewy glow.

"Good thing I was here to catch you instead of in my SUV heading back to town," he said, smiling down at her as he kept his hands securely on her shoulders.

A muscle twitched in her jaw but she didn't crack a smile. "You think you're charming, don't you?"

"He is charming," Aunt Miranda piped up. "Don't you think Cole is charming, Julie?"

"Definitely," Julie said, nodding.

"I'm a guy and even I think he's charming," Drew interjected.

"You think so, too, don't you, Anna?" Julie asked.

Cole tilted his head as he waited for her answer. She seemed to war with herself before she snapped, "Yes."

They continued walking. The night was freezing, with a stiff breeze blowing from the west, but Cole wouldn't have been surprised had steam come from under Anna's hat.

"Why are you so angry?" he whispered in a voice low enough that only she could hear.

"Because I really do think you're charming," she retorted, keeping her voice down. "Wanting you off this mountain would be a heck of a lot easier if you weren't."

"Sorry about that," he said, but hid a smile.

Her candor was just so darn refreshing, especially because he'd dated a string of women who wouldn't say what was on their minds unless their makeup was being held hostage.

The last woman he'd gone out with before leaving San Diego had a standard reply every time he tried to elicit her opinion.

"Whatever you say, Cole."

Her constant compliance had driven him crazy. Not that Anna couldn't make him crazy, too. But she tended to affect his nerve endings more than his nerves.

He shoved his hands in his pockets, perhaps more to stop himself from reaching for Anna than because they were cold. Although, after living in southern California for most of his life, he wasn't fond of having fingers the temperature of Popsicles.

"What are you two lovebirds talking about back there?" Miranda called over her shoulder.

"How many times do I have to tell you that we're not lovebirds, Aunt Miranda?" Anna asked in an exasperated voice.

"You're not?" Miranda put one hand to her breast. "You should do something about that, Anna. I recommend trying out the hot tub on the deck back at the chalet. I hear making love in one is a transcendental experience."

"That sounds like something we should do," Julie told Drew excitedly.

"I'm there," Drew said, tightening the arm he had draped around his wife.

"Once again, Miranda, you take the prize for lack of tact," remarked Peter, who was walking six feet to the right of his wife. Bits of snow clung to his dark beard. "Can't you be discreet?"

"What's to be discreet about?" Miranda asked with asperity. "It's not like I'm speaking from experience. The only way you'd go in our hot tub is if I had it transported to your office."

"You know how demanding my job is, Miranda," Peter said in a low voice. "And this is not the right time to talk about it."

"It's never the right time," Miranda said and stalked off, her high-heeled black boots making sharp indentations in the snow. Cole expected Peter to give chase but instead he sent the rest of them an embarrassed smile. "Sorry about that. I don't know what gets into her sometimes."

Cole could take a pretty good guess, but he had his own female problems to worry about. Namely the five feet eight of simmering woman at his side. Too bad he was pretty sure the simmering had more to do with anger than desire.

When they reached the chalet a few minutes later, he was seriously considering the possibility that he'd miscalculated.

What if Anna wasn't as attracted to him as he was to her?

What if she truly didn't want to embark on the affair he had in mind?

What if she dreaded sharing a room with him rather than looking forward to it?

"Hey, buddy, could you do me a favor?" Drew said in a low voice as he sidled up to him.

"Sure," Cole said.

"Stay out of the hot tub tonight, okay? If this is as good as I think it will be, we can work out a schedule for tomorrow."

Julie was whispering in Anna's ear, ostensibly the same thing judging by the color that crept up Anna's neck.

"Sure, pal," he told Drew a moment before the other man grabbed his wife by the hand and headed for the second floor of the chalet, which opened into a wraparound deck complete with hot tub.

"Looks like Miranda has already turned in," Cole remarked to Peter and Anna when he noticed the older woman was nowhere to be seen.

"She always goes to sleep before I do," Peter said as he removed his coat and boots. "Hope you two don't mind if I monopolize the downstairs. It helps if I have total quiet when I work."

"I don't know about Cole, but I'm going straight to sleep," Anna said.

She slanted Cole a cross look, probably to convey she didn't have anything other than sleep in mind. Then she ran lightly up the steps toward their bedroom.

Cole followed after a few moments, wishing he was headed for the hot tub instead. Too bad Anna didn't seem as though she'd be amenable to joining him in the heated, frothing water anytime soon.

ANNA SPLASHED COOL WATER on her face to counteract the heat of her temper. She dabbed at the moisture with a towel before examining her reflection in the ornate bathroom mirror.

Sparks of temper lit her eyes and lent a rosy glow to her skin, making her look like she was spoiling for a good fight. She heard the door leading from the hallway to the bedroom open then close.

Good. Her opponent had arrived.

He was probably stretching out on the bed, artfully arranging himself so she'd take one look at him and launch herself into his strong, muscular arms. No doubt he was proud of himself for realizing the intellectual beefcake thing he had going on appealed to her.

"How dare he assume I'll sleep with him simply because he's irresistible," she said to her irate reflection.

Fueled by her temper, she wrenched open the bathroom door, prepared to resist the sexy tableau of man and bed.

But both twin beds were empty. Cole stood at the cedar-lined closet with his back to her.

"What are you doing?" she asked.

He didn't turn around, but reached for something on a high shelf in the closet. "Gathering sheets and a blanket. I thought I'd go downstairs and make up the sofa."

Anna put her hands on her hips. The man was absolutely maddening. "What kind of new strategy is this?"

"I don't know what you mean," he said. When he turned around, he had a stack of pale-pink sheets and a darker pink blanket in his arms. Instead of making him appear ridiculous, the color emphasized his dark good looks.

"You. Saying you'll sleep on the sofa. What gives?"

"I'm not following you."

"Oh, come on. I was there last night when you kissed me. Why are you offering to sleep on the sofa when we both know you want to sleep with me?"

To her surprise, he smiled. It wasn't a small grin but a wide, unabashed smile that stretched his lips wide. "You don't mince words, do you?"

"Am I wrong?" she demanded.

He shook his head. "Maybe a little misguided but not wrong. I don't push myself on women who don't want me."

Not want him? Where had he gotten that idea?

"Weren't you listening when I told you the story about the potbellied pig?" she asked. "Of course I want you. That's not the issue."

He cocked an eyebrow and gave her a very male grin.

"I don't know about that. You want me. I want you. Sounds to me like that should be the issue."

"The issue," she continued before he could expand on what he could probably convince her was a very good case, "is that you came up here uninvited."

"Julie invited me."

She jabbed an accusatory index finger at him. "After I told you loud and clear that we couldn't have a relationship outside of work."

"You did say that," he agreed as he moved away from the closet. For one crazy second, she thought he'd sweep her into his arms as easily as he swept away her protests. But he merely laid the bedclothes on the edge of one of the twin beds.

"Problem is you didn't ask my opinion," he said when his hands were empty.

Although she had a terrible premonition she wouldn't like the answer, she still couldn't resist asking the question. "What is your opinion?"

He removed his glasses, taking his time as he deliberately cleaned the lenses with the edge of his sweater. Without them, he was even more of a looker. His lashes were long and thick and the blue of his eyes so rich she could detect the color from the width of the room away. She waited impatiently while he settled the glasses back on the bridge of his nose.

"I think we should have an affair," he said finally.

She closed her eyes against the wave of heat that overtook her. Figuring she was no match for it, she gave in and sat down on the edge of her bed.

Never taking his eyes from her, he sat down himself.

His tawny skin and nearly black hair contrasted with the rose-colored bedspread and called attention to his good looks.

He leaned forward, put his elbows on his knees and dangled his hands between his legs. "Can I take it from that reaction that you're considering it?"

Her eyes snapped open. "No, I am *not* considering it."

His lips flattened. "You said not five minutes ago that you want me."

"I also said that wanting you is a problem for me." She sighed. "I admit it. You're hot. But you're not just any hot guy. You're the hot guy I work with. I can't sleep with you."

He was silent for no more than a second. "Okay."

"Okay?" she repeated. Had he actually said that? Temper took the place of the desire churning inside her. "What do you mean by okay?"

He shrugged. "I mean okay. I accept that."

She narrowed her eyes. "Did you hear me say I couldn't sleep with you?"

"Yep," he said cheerfully. He got up, picked up the bedclothes and crossed to the closet.

"What are you doing now?" Anna asked.

"Putting away this stuff," he said as he crammed the sheets and blanket back into the closet.

"But I thought you were sleeping on the sofa." Anna meant for her voice to sound harsh but instead it came out soft.

"No reason we can't sleep in the same room now." He brushed his hands together after completing the task. "You can trust me, Anna. I'd never take liberties with a woman after she said she didn't want to sleep with me."

Anna's mouth dropped open. It was on the tip of her tongue to point out once again that she *wouldn't* sleep with him, not that she didn't *want* to.

"What's wrong?" he asked. She would have bought his act of innocence if his lips hadn't curled in an impish grin. "Don't tell me you don't trust yourself to be in the same room with me."

"Of course I don't," she bit out, and he laughed.

"Tell you what. You take the bed you're on, and I'll sleep in the other one."

Without warning, he pulled his thick sweater over his head and tossed it on the bed. His fingers went to the buttons on the cream-colored dress shirt he wore under the sweater.

"What do you think you're doing now?" she asked, her voice cracking.

"Undressing," he said. "I don't know about you, but I find it hard to sleep in my clothes."

He went to work on the buttons and she braced herself for a glimpse of his naked chest. Instead she saw the white of his T-shirt. Her breath expelled in a relieved whoosh, but caught again when he shrugged out of his button-down shirt.

The T-shirt clung to his massive chest, delineating his musculature. She'd known he was an impressive physical specimen, but saw that he was even more of an Adonis than she'd supposed.

His broad shoulders tapered down to a flawlessly

shaped chest that featured bulging pectoral muscles before narrowing to a proportionately small waist.

She prayed her mouth wasn't gaping open in awe.

Say something, she told herself. *Say something or he'll get the wrong idea.*

"With a build like that, you must spend a lot of time in the gym," was what escaped her lips.

She closed her eyes in mortification. She might as well have said what was really on her mind: Wowza!

"Some," he said, "but I have mostly genetics to thank for my build. The men in my family are naturally muscular."

"Oh," Anna said inanely.

He crossed to the bathroom, one of his hands at the snap at the waistband of his winter-weight jeans. "I hope you don't mind if we turn out the lights soon," he called to her. "I got up early today and I'm wiped."

Anna had risen early, too. The ski resort was a two-hour drive from her townhouse, and they'd wanted to get a jump on lift traffic, which tended to be heavy over the holidays. Cole, on the other hand, hadn't showed up at White Tower until after dark.

"Why did you get up early?" she asked.

His back was to her, but she sensed from his pause that he didn't want to answer.

"No reason in particular. I just had things to do."

He closed the bathroom door behind him before she could ask him to elaborate, not that she didn't have a pretty good guess already.

He'd been working.

She hadn't assigned him any long-term projects so

she could only assume he'd devised some way to best her, possibly with new marketing ideas. Maybe he even intended to bypass her and pitch them directly to Mr. Skillington.

She spied his black leather briefcase in the spot where he'd dropped it. Would it be so wrong to take a peek inside? She was his boss. Who could blame her for wanting to know what he was working on?

She was barely aware that her brain had signaled her legs to move until she was standing over his bed, against which the briefcase lay propped. She bent to reach for it but froze when the bathroom door opened.

"What are you doing?" Cole asked.

She jerked upright, her mind springing into action.

"I'm—" She took the remaining step to his bed and let herself fall onto it. Her butt bounced once, then stilled. "Testing out which bed is firmer. I love a hard..."

She made the mistake of looking at him and what she'd been about to say died on her lips. He still wore the white T-shirt but he no longer had on his jeans.

A pair of red silk boxer shorts he'd probably gotten for Christmas covered the essential part of him but left his very long, very muscular legs bare.

She blinked. She'd hadn't seen better calf definition since watching the Olympic sprinters compete in the hundred-meter dash. Cole's legs were more impressive. He was like one of those sprinters with fifty percent more body mass.

"You love a hard what?" he asked, moving across the room like a predator.

Body, her mind screamed.

"Mattress," she said in a small voice. "I love a hard mattress."

His grin started slow and spread. His gaze dipped below her neck and roamed. He sat down on the bed next to her so that his mostly-bare thigh brushed her body.

He skimmed a single fingertip down her cheek, pausing at the center of her chin before tracing downward so that it rested in the hollow of her neck. A pulse there beat madly.

"I like soft things," he said in a silky voice.

He'd removed his glasses while in the bathroom, and his eyes were so blue it was difficult for her to take a breath, as though she were drowning in them.

She tore her eyes from his and scrambled off the bed, astonished that he'd set her on fire with the touch of a mere fingertip. If he could do that, imagine what other parts of him could do to her.

She closed her eyes, trying to shut off her imagination. It didn't help. Do something, she thought. Anything to stop thinking about the unequaled pleasures he could show her in bed. She suppressed a groan and quickly gathered the supplies she needed for bed, being careful to avoid his eyes.

She hurried for the bathroom on unsteady legs. Behind her, she could hear the rustle of sheets as he turned back the bed covers. A question burned in her mind. She was almost to the door of the bathroom when she could no longer contain it.

"Have you, um, finished undressing for the night?" she asked, not daring to look at him.

"If you're asking if I sleep nude, the answer's yes. But not tonight." The rest of his reply came in a sexy, low-throated whisper. "I won't do anything tonight you don't want me to do."

She rushed into the bathroom without replying, leaning weakly against the door once she was in relative safety. She fanned herself but the brush of air did nothing to dispel the heat firing her body.

She was amazed that Cole still didn't get it.

Wanting him had nothing to do with not being able to have him.

6

COLE STAMPED HIS FEET to keep the circulation moving in his toes, thinking Anna looked cute when she rolled her eyes. Even if she directed the eye roll at him.

"I can't believe you didn't tell me you couldn't ski," Anna said for at least the third time since they'd gotten in the long line at the ski lift.

The snow was falling so heavily that it nearly blanketed the sky in a cloud of white, which had made any discussion of Cole leaving White Tower today superfluous.

He'd wager Anna wasn't too happy about that.

"I did tell you," he countered.

"Not until we were at the cashier's window and she asked what kind of lift ticket you wanted. You could have told me this morning."

He thought back to breakfast, which he, Miranda and Anna had eaten in silence. Drew and Julie had chattered happily in what Cole assumed was post-hot-tub bliss. Peter hadn't bothered to show up at all.

"You weren't in the best mood," he pointed out.

"Neither were you."

"I'm not the one who decided we should sleep in separate beds."

"I'm not the one at a ski resort without a clue how to ski," she snapped back.

That stung. He guessed she hadn't awarded him bonus points for being an instant expert on snowplowing, which involved putting the tips of the skis together in order to slow down.

"You didn't have to offer to teach me," he said.

"There wasn't a ski school this morning. What was I supposed to do? Leave you on your own so you could fall down and kill yourself?"

She crossed her arms over the zippered front of a fashionable lightweight teal ski jacket that complemented her brown hair and olive skin. Cole thought she looked more beautiful than any of the models his father used in the advertisements for Skillington Ski.

"Why can't you ski anyway?" she asked.

"Southern California boy, remember? I prefer the beach."

"But then why apply for a job at Skillington?" She seemed completely mystified. "Why aren't you marketing something you know about?"

It was a very good question. Cole's passion was cycling, which had led to his last job in the marketing department of a large, all-purpose bike shop. He'd eventually outgrown the job but not his love for the product.

Arthur Skillington, however, didn't sell bicycles.

Cole made himself shrug. "You don't have to personally experience something to successfully market it."

"How do you figure?"

"Ever see that commercial on TV for liver-rich cat

food? I'm betting whoever dreamed up that campaign never sampled what he's selling."

"No, but he probably has a cat."

Cole indicated his all-mountain carving skis and lightweight composite ski poles. "I have ski equipment."

"Equipment you barely know how to use," she said with a sigh in her voice. "Are you sure you're ready to tackle something besides the bunny hill?"

He tucked a strand of her dark hair back in her cap, pleased at the way she sucked in a breath when his fingers brushed her face.

"For a woman who professes not to want me around," he said softly, "you're awfully concerned about my safety."

She swatted his hand away.

"Look," she said. "I know it must seem like my defenses are weakening toward you, but nothing sexual is going to happen between us on this vacation."

"So you've said." He brushed his knuckles over her cheek, listening to the way her breathing went ragged. "Over and over."

She stepped back from him. "I'm saying it again so you'll stop touching me."

He leaned toward her. "Does it bother you when I touch you?"

"Yes," she hissed. "You don't notice me grabbing you, do you?"

"There you are, Anna. I've been looking all over for you."

A handsome, compactly built man who was probably

in his mid-thirties stood to one side of them, having approached as silently as an arctic cat.

"Brad," Anna exclaimed, then grabbed Cole's right arm and hung on. She directed what seemed like a false smile at the new arrival. "What are you doing here?"

"I already told you." Brad answered her but watched Cole with narrowed, assessing eyes. "Looking for you. Your parents told me you'd be at White Tower this week."

Cole immediately made the connection. Anna's mother had mentioned a Brad Perriman on Christmas Eve, expressing a dashed hope that Anna would date him. Judging by the way she'd captured his arm and wouldn't let go, Anna hadn't changed her mind about not wanting to go out with Brad.

"Did my parents tell you about Cole?" she asked, squeezing his arm. Cole waited for her to claim they were involved but the pressure on his arm decreased and her voice deflated. "Cole and I work together."

Brad's expression lightened, which wasn't acceptable. Cole didn't know why Anna had lost her nerve but his course of action was clear.

"That's how we met." Cole dropped a kiss on Anna's forehead and tightened his arm around shoulders that suddenly felt stiff. A shadow seemed to pass over Brad's face. "I'm Cole Mansfield. And you are?"

"Dr. Brad Perriman." He looked unhappily from one of them to the other. "I got the impression from Anna's parents that she'd be up here...unattached."

"Nope. She's attached to me." He ignored Anna's sharply indrawn breath and gathered her even closer.

"Rosemary and Bob never mentioned you," Brad said.

"Probably because I met them for the first time on Christmas Eve," Cole said. "Anna and I were pretty quiet about what was happening between us until then. Weren't we, darling?"

She elbowed him in the ribs, but his sappy endearment did the job. The corners of Brad's mouth tugged downward and he nodded shortly at Anna.

"I guess I'll see you around," he said, then was gone.

"Why did you do that?" Anna asked the second Brad was out of hearing range.

He released a short breath, which was visible in the cool air. "Correct me if I'm wrong, but I got the impression you were trying to brush this guy off."

"I was," she exclaimed, then threw up her hands, "but I didn't want you to lie to him."

"I didn't lie."

"You let him think something was going on between us!"

"You were going to do the same thing."

"I changed my mind when I realized how dishonest it was."

"It's not dishonest," he said, bringing his head nearer to hers. "Something is going on between us, whether you like it or not."

"But Brad thinks we're together."

"We slept in the same room last night, and we're standing beside each other in this lift line. In my book, that means we *are* together."

She shook her head in exasperation. "We're not together the way he thinks we are."

He took her by the shoulders. "What does it matter if it gets him to stay away from you? That's what you want, right?"

She slanted a look over her shoulder at Brad, who was about ten skiers behind them. The line was moving slowly, giving him plenty of time to watch them and draw his own conclusions about their relationship.

"He won't take no for an answer. He told my father he was divorced but I found out from a mutual friend that he's not even separated."

"Have you told your dad that?"

She shook her head. "They're colleagues. I didn't want to damage their professional relationship. I figured I'd handle him myself. After all, I have lots of experience in dealing with men like him."

"What do you mean, men like him?"

"Liars. Let's just say I haven't been fortunate enough to meet many trustworthy men," she explained. He winced, but again rationalized that he wasn't technically lying to her. He was being loyal to his father. "But no matter how many times I tell Brad I don't want to date him, he thinks I'll change my mind," she continued, then blew out a breath. "He's so pushy, he might not even give up now. Not when he sees us arguing."

"Then let's not argue," Cole suggested, tracing a finger across her lower lip. With his gloves shoved in his pockets, his fingers were nearly frozen but he thought it was worth risking frostbite to touch her.

"Anna," he said softly.

"Huh?" Her dark eyes had gone wide.

"It's our turn to get on the ski lift."

Anna's eyes cleared and she briskly shuffled forward to the loading point, looking over her outside shoulder for the approaching chair. Cole did the same, although he didn't hold on to the seat with his free hand and as a result sat down with a hard plop.

"You are *so* not a skier," she said, giggling when she had the safety bar lowered and their skis dangled in the air.

"Brad's watching," Cole said after checking the line. "Now's our chance."

"Chance to do what?"

"To do this," he said before cupping her head with his free hand and kissing her.

He wasn't sure whether the feeling in his stomach was because of the chair lifting or his soul soaring. Her lips were soft and malleable, so different from the ones that repeatedly told him she couldn't get involved with him.

It was far too late to warn him off now, he thought as they ascended into the sky. Snow blew around them and wind rushed over their legs, but the overwhelming sensation was of a warm liquid heat that settled in his groin.

How hard would it be for a beginner, he wondered, to ski with a burgeoning erection?

Uncaring of the answer, he slanted his head, deepening the kiss, frustrated by the layers of clothes that made it impossible to touch her beautiful body.

They were both panting and out of breath when they drew apart.

"You didn't need to do that," she said, her words so soft they were nearly carried away by the rush of wind. "Brad couldn't have caught more than the first couple of seconds."

"I didn't kiss you for Brad," he said loudly enough that she could hear. It was important that she hear. "I kissed you for me."

He waited, hoping for a similar admission. The seconds ticked by so quickly as she stared back at him that he was shocked when she lifted the safety bar, signaling to him that they were approaching the unloading area.

"Lift the tips of your skis," Anna told him.

He did as she said and felt the backs of his skis touch down on the off ramp. He stood up and tried to push himself forward and away from the chair.

His skis shot out from under him and he fell hard on his rear end, traveling over the snow like a baseball player sliding into second base. He saw stars for an instant before the people behind him started to embark.

He scrambled out of the way, losing a ski in the process, and finally looked up into Anna's beautiful, concerned face.

"Are you hurt?" she asked anxiously.

"Only my pride," he answered before the ghost of a smile appeared on her face. To her credit, she didn't laugh. She did, however, glance toward a ski run he suddenly suspected was far beyond his capability.

"Too bad you can't ski as well as you can kiss," she said impishly before putting out a hand to help him up.

His rear end still hurt, but his pride was immeasurably better even as he realized it was going to be a long, hard day on the slopes.

"SO WHAT HAPPENED after he fell off the chairlift?" Julie asked, popping a couple kernels of popcorn into her mouth as she snuggled under Drew's arm on the sofa in the chalet.

Anna slanted Cole a questioning look, silently asking for permission to tell the entire story. He rolled his eyes before nodding at her, like the good sport he'd been all day.

"Go ahead and tell her," he said, rubbing a spot on his hip she was sure must be sore. "I can't get any more humiliated than I was out there on the slope."

"So then he asks me if he can snowplow the entire way down the hill," Anna said, leaning forward on the sofa in her eagerness to give the story justice.

"I did not," Cole said, then grimaced. He ran a hand through his hair. "I asked if I needed to make those fancy turns she told me about. There's a difference."

She cast him a laughing look. "I tell him snowplowing wouldn't be a good idea. He needs to do the turns. About then, a group of little kids who had been with us on the bunny hill gets off the lift and passes by us."

"They weren't that little," Cole protested.

"The oldest one had dinosaurs on his ski jacket and a cartoon mouse on his helmet," Anna said.

"Go on," Drew said, reaching forward to take a handful of popcorn. Julie did the same, her eyes riveted on Anna and Cole.

"This little kid says to Cole, 'What's your problem, mister? Are you turkey?'"

"Turkey?" Julie screwed up her face. "What does that mean?"

"I believe he meant to ask if I was chicken," Cole supplied, earning laughter all around.

"Then Cole gets this determined look on his face and heads down the run behind the posse of little kids, only he's making these sharp turns instead of the slow, gentle ones I told him to." Anna's voice picked up steam as she continued the story. "He starts going faster and faster until he sees Dinosaur Boy about thirty yards in front of him."

"It was more like ten," Cole said.

"Like I said, the kid was thirty yards in front of him. And I yell, 'That's it, Cole. You're doing it. You're skiing!'"

"Then what happened?" Julie asked and shoved another half-dozen popcorn kernels into her mouth.

"Then his knees bend and his butt drops and his arms go all akimbo. One of his skis flies in the air and the other veers to his side and slides down the mountain. I ski up to him, worried he's broken something. He looks up at me, and do you know what he says?"

"No, what?" Drew asked, transfixed.

"That kid made me do it."

Drew and Julie laughed. Cole made a grab for Anna, gently pulling her against him. She felt the rumble of his good-natured laughter against her back.

"So you thought that was funny?" he asked beside her ear.

"Only 'cause it was," she said, giggling so hard her eyes watered.

"You made it down the run okay, right?" Julie asked when the laughter in the room had subsided to a more manageable level. "You didn't fall again?"

"Hell, yeah, I fell again," Cole said. "About five more times. That's when I suggested Anna might want to take a couple runs without me. I spent the rest of the afternoon by the fireplace in the lodge watching football and drinking hot chocolate."

"And when I had enough of the snow," Anna finished, "I joined him for dinner." She curled her legs up under her, content to nestle against Cole's solid warmth. "We didn't see either of you on the slopes. What did you two newlyweds do today?"

Julie and Drew exchanged a conspiratorial look, shared laughter and a quick kiss.

"Never mind," Anna said. "I can guess."

"How about Miranda and Peter?" Cole asked. "We didn't see them either."

No sooner had her name been mentioned than Miranda strolled into the room, looking cool and composed in black leggings and a rich aqua sweater. Her hair was immaculately done, and she was drinking what appeared to be a martini.

"Peter spent the day working, as usual." The ice cubes in Miranda's drink clinked against each other as she sat down. "I got my hair and nails done, then treated myself to a lobster dinner."

"With Uncle Peter?" Julie asked.

"I believe your uncle is having dinner as we speak," Miranda said, then took a healthy swallow of her drink. "By the way, Anna and Cole, I moved your things into the bedroom Peter and I used last night."

"Don't worry. I put on fresh sheets and moved all our things out of the room."

"But why?" Anna asked as panic started to take hold in her chest.

"Because your room has twin beds. The one I moved you into has a king. You're bound to get far more... enjoyment out of it than your uncle and I."

LATER THAT NIGHT, Cole leaned one shoulder against the door frame, balancing a different set of bedsheets in his arms than he had the night before. He raised a dark eyebrow at Anna, causing her pulse to jump.

There was something about that man and cotton sheets that got to her.

"Just so we have this straight, I don't have any objection to sharing that bed with you." He nodded toward the king-sized sleigh bed in the center of their new, more spacious room. "The only reason I offered to sleep on the sofa again was to win points with you."

"You did." Anna smiled at him. "To tell you the truth, you've been winning points all day."

"Then I better go," he said, smiling back. "You never know when I'll have enough points to claim the prize."

When he was gone, Anna figured she was supposed to deduce from his parting comment that she was the prize.

If Cole had said something like that just yesterday, she'd have taken offense. But she found herself humming as she went through her nightly preparations for bed. She changed into a short silk nightgown, thankful to eschew last night's modest cotton T-shirt.

She slipped into bed, got under the sheets and turned out the lights, honest enough to admit she wasn't sure she could have resisted Cole had he been with her.

She, Cole, Julie, and Drew had stayed downstairs talking and drinking wine until almost eleven. They'd spent most of the time laughing, partly because Cole had been such a good sport about being a rotten skier.

The more time she spent with him, in fact, the more she liked him. He was open and honest, a refreshing change from what she had begun to think was the norm.

Ever since college, when her boyfriend's late-night study sessions turned out to involve his exploration of the anatomy of various coeds, Anna had been slow to trust.

Her heart had come away from the incident relatively unscathed, but she'd vowed to be more careful in the future. But no matter how hard she tried to avoid them, she kept running across men who lied to get their way.

Brad Perriman and Larry Lipinski were classic examples. Cole, however, seemed to be an exception: that rare, honest man.

He also had a body impressive enough to make a nun salivate. She wiped at the corner of her mouth, surprised not to find any moisture there. Then she swallowed. Just in case.

She fanned herself, giggled, then said aloud, "Somebody needs to knock some sense into you, girl."

At the sound of three soft knocks, she nearly fell out of bed. Belatedly realizing somebody was in the hall outside the room, she sat up at the same time the door opened.

Cole walked in, a large soft blur in the darkness.

"I hope I didn't wake you, but the sofa's occupied," he said. "Peter got to it before I did. I would have come upstairs sooner but he started talking stock market index futures and I couldn't get away."

Because that was one of Uncle Peter's pet subjects, Anna knew the trapped feeling. But her uncle's obsession with the stock market didn't explain why he wasn't sleeping with Aunt Miranda...or perhaps it did.

"The problems he and Aunt Miranda are having must be more serious than I thought," she mused.

Cole closed the door, casting the room in darkness. Anna automatically switched on a light, which caused her pupils to constrict. She blinked, trying to adjust to the sudden brightness. When she could see normally again, she realized Cole hadn't moved.

"Cole?" she began, then noticed that his jaw had gone slack and his powerful chest was expanding and contracting more rapidly than usual. He was staring directly at her chest.

Her hand flew to the thin material that barely covered her and she realized his hungry stare had been enough to pebble her nipples. She hastily pulled the bedsheet up to her neck.

His sigh was so loud she heard it clear across the room.

"I'd suggest you sleep in the same room as your aunt if your uncle hadn't mentioned the door was locked," he said.

When she didn't reply, he set the sheets down on the floor and began arranging the blanket flat on the carpet.

"You don't mean to sleep on the floor," she cried. It was too cold, too uncomfortable.

He raised his dark head. "Unless you've changed your mind about sleeping with me, I don't have much choice."

She bit her lip, hoping she wouldn't regret her next words. "It's silly for you to sleep on the floor when we have a king-sized bed. Tell you what. You stay on your side, I'll stay on mine and we'll just...sleep."

He cocked one dark eyebrow doubtfully. "Are you sure?"

"No," she said. "But I'm willing to give it a try if you are."

"Okay," he said through teeth that sounded as though they were clamped together.

Anticipating that he'd strip down to what he'd worn to bed the night before, she turned her head. No need to tempt herself with another eyeful of gorgeous hunk. She heard him setting his glasses down on the night table and waited until the mattress depressed from his weight to turn out the lights.

"Good night, Cole."

There was a pause before he answered, "Good night, Anna."

The rustle of sheets as he settled in for the night sounded inordinately loud in the quiet of the room. She tried unsuccessfully to get her body to relax. Her mind was a hopeless cause. It was racing.

Although she couldn't see a thing in the darkness, it was all too easy to call up an image of his magnificent body lying just feet away from her. Close enough that she could reach out and touch him if she turned to one side.

She held herself perfectly still, afraid of what would happen if she fell asleep. What if they turned at the same time during the night? What if they ended up entwined? What if sleep dulled their inhibitions?

Her breaths seemed too loud so she tried to slow them. In. Out. In. Out. She'd been dead on her feet only fifteen minutes before. Why wasn't she sleepy now?

Five minutes passed. Ten. Twenty.

"Anna?" The low timbre of Cole's voice penetrated the darkness. "You're awake, aren't you?"

She hesitated, then figured it was pointless to pretend to be asleep. "Yes," she said.

"I'm having a hard time getting to sleep."

"Me, too," she admitted.

"It was hard for me fall asleep last night, too. I couldn't stop thinking about how close you were and how much I wanted to make love to you."

Anna shut her eyes against the sudden onslaught on her senses, but the liquid sensation flowed through her body like honey. Sometimes honesty wasn't the best policy, but she was as wedded to it as he seemed to be. Her confession was inevitable.

"Me, too."

She heard movement, as though he'd propped himself on one elbow. "What do you propose we do about it?" he asked in a voice so low and sexy a shudder passed through her.

Anna wet her lips.

"I think," she said, "that we should talk."

7

"TALK?" COLE PRAYED his hearing had gone bad but knew with a sinking certainty that his ears worked just fine. He'd hinted at seduction and she'd suggested conversation. He swallowed, trying not to let frustration overwhelm him. "Okay, fine. What do you want to talk about?"

"Are you a body builder?"

He rubbed his forehead with his thumb and two fingers. How was he supposed to get his mind off what his body wanted when she'd made his physique a topic of discussion?

"Can't say that I am." He tried to make it seem as though the question were perfectly appropriate. "I work out at the gym a couple times a week but that's as far as it goes."

"I've seen guys who work out at the gym and very few of them look as good as you do."

He blew out an agonized breath. "Anna, do you really think telling me you like my body will get our minds off sex?"

"Sorry," she whispered. "I was curious, that's all. About the muscles, I mean. Not the sex."

That hurt. "You're not curious about the sex?"

"Of course I'm curious."

Her admission made him want to bury himself in her so badly that he could barely think, but he couldn't help but chuckle at her frank answer.

"Curious isn't the word I'd use," he said. "I'd go with something like craving."

"Could you please stick to the topic?" she asked, but her voice sounded more shaky than irritated. Good.

"What was the topic?"

"How you can barely work out and still look like that."

"I guess it's mostly genetics," he said, thinking about Arthur Skillington. His father had been a defensive lineman for the University of Pittsburgh. So, too, had his grandfather. "I come from a long line of football linemen."

"If you have athletic genes, how come you can't ski?"

"I'd probably be an okay skier if I worked at it." He gave a self-deprecating chuckle. "That is, if I got over the fact that my center of gravity is so much higher than most people's. But, to be honest, the sport doesn't appeal to me."

"You mean, not like football. Where did you play?"

"I didn't."

"But you just said…" Her voice lost steam as she considered that. "Why didn't you play football?"

The answer was more complicated than she realized, but he could give her the simple version. "Probably because my mom wasn't into sports. She wanted me to use my brain instead of my brawn."

"How about your dad?"

Because he assumed she was asking about the father

who raised him, he answered, "He's a nuclear physicist. He used to take me to scientific exhibits instead of ball games."

"Why didn't you become a scientist, then?"

Cole put his hands behind his head and settled back against the pillow. Talking hadn't yet taken the edge off wanting, and he figured he'd be less tempted to reach for her this way.

"You wouldn't ask that if you'd heard nuclear fusion explained as many times as I have," Cole said. "My father's a great guy. Unfortunately, he suffers from a terminal disease."

"Oh, no," Anna cried. "What's wrong with him?"

"He's boring."

She giggled. "You're bad."

"Nope, just truthful. Ask my mom. She'll tell you."

"It doesn't bother your mom that he's a bore?"

"Are you kidding? We're talking about a woman whose idea of a big night on the town is a trip to a twenty-four hour grocery store."

"You're not saying your mom's a bore, too, are you?"

"No, I'm not," he said while something softened in his heart. His mother had made mistakes in her life, one in particular a whopper, but he'd never doubted her love for him. "She's wonderful."

"You had to tell me that, didn't you?" she said on a groan. "You must know there are few things more appealing than a man with a soft spot for his mother."

He laughed. "In my case, it's true. Although if you want to use that as an excuse to ravish me, go right ahead."

"We're talking, remember? Not ravishing," she said in a mock-stern voice.

"In the condition I'm in," he said wryly, shifting slightly to make himself more comfortable, "that's impossible to forget."

"When did your parents get divorced?" she asked.

"They're not divorced," he said without thinking.

"But you said you have two sets of parents, that your father lives around Pittsburgh."

Oh, what a tangled web we weave, when first we practice to deceive. Sir Walter Scott's quote ran through Cole's mind, although he'd neither set out to deceive Anna nor lie to her. Not in the strictest sense.

"My second father lives in Pittsburgh," he said, then sensed her confusion. "It's a long story."

"I'd like to hear it," she offered, a request that left him speechless. A few seconds ticked by. "I mean, if you want to tell me. If you don't want to, that's okay, too."

He shouldn't tell her, not when Arthur Skillington was a major part of the story. He hadn't shared the tale with anyone else, not even his childhood friends in San Diego. He hadn't made sense of it yet himself.

But the words were tapping against the backs of his teeth, wanting to get out. If he was careful not to refer to Arthur Skillington by name, maybe he could let them.

"It's not easy to talk about," he said, still surprised that he wanted to. "The thing is I didn't know I had a father in Pittsburgh until seven months ago."

"You're adopted, aren't you?" she guessed.

Although it was too dark to see more than the glowing face of the alarm clock and the faint outline of her expression, he felt her eyes on him.

"I think this is a case of too many people wanting me instead of not enough. Except my biological father didn't get a chance to claim me until recently." He swallowed, because it was difficult to make the next admission aloud. "My mother never told him she was pregnant."

"That's terrible," Anna exclaimed, then shut her mouth so fast he could hear her teeth tap together. "I'm sorry. I shouldn't have said that. I know she's your mother and she must have had a good reason but—"

"But depriving your son of his father is a rotten thing to do," he finished for her. "Believe me, I agree with you."

"You've forgiven her, haven't you?"

"I said I didn't agree with what she did, not that I didn't understand it. At the time, I think it seemed to her like she was doing the right thing."

He expected to have difficulty getting the story out, but to his surprise the next words flowed.

"When she was nineteen, she flew to Pittsburgh to be a bridesmaid in the wedding of a girl she'd gone to high school with in California. My dad—my biological dad, that is—was a friend of the groom. He was a college football player: Big, athletic, handsome. And she was a pretty girl enjoying being away from home for the first time. They ended up in bed together. After the wedding, my mom flew back to San Diego."

"It couldn't have been too hard to find him when she discovered she was pregnant," Anna interjected.

"Probably not, but by that time she was in love with the dad who raised me. He said it didn't matter that the baby wasn't his and asked her to marry him. They convinced themselves it wouldn't be so terrible not to tell my real dad about the pregnancy. I've had a harder time accepting that they didn't tell *me*."

He fell silent, thinking about the decision that had changed the fabric of his life. He grew up wanting for nothing, in particular love, but a few months with Arthur Skillington had proved his first twenty-nine years would have been richer had he been in them.

"But how did you find out?"

"By mistake." This part of the story was especially hard to revisit, but Cole had gotten this far so he kept talking. "My father, the one in San Diego, needed knee replacement surgery for his arthritic knee.

"Have I mentioned he's as quirky as they come? Deathly afraid of needles, worried sick about the safety of the nation's blood supply. It freaked him out that he would need a transfusion after surgery.

"I'd heard about directed transfusions but I wasn't sure whether our blood was compatible so I didn't want to get his hopes up for nothing. I went to the hospital and asked to be tested to see if I could donate blood for him."

During the story, Anna had gravitated to his side of the bed so that she was only inches from him. Her hand, small and slim, reached out and squeezed his. The gesture gave him the strength to continue.

"My blood is type AB," he said. "Turns out he's type O."

He heard her soft gasp and knew she understood.

"It's impossible for a person with AB blood to have a parent who's type O," Anna finished for him, moving even closer.

"Bingo," Cole said. "Instant second father."

She laid her head on his shoulder. "Your second father must have been just as shocked as you were when he found out."

Cole thought of the way his palms had sweat and his voice shook in that initial phone call to Arthur Skillington. Because he'd been born almost nine months to the day after the wedding where his parents had met, Cole hadn't been afraid his father wouldn't believe him. He'd feared Skillington wouldn't want to know him.

"He was understandably angry at my mother and more than a little shocked," Cole said. "But shocked in a good way. He was a bachelor for a long time because he thought he didn't want to be a husband. Turned out he always wanted a son."

"He sounds wonderful," Anna said. "I'd like to meet him one day."

The knowledge that she already had met Arthur Skillington—in fact, worked for him—was like a spear through Cole's heart. Even as Anna trustingly snuggled against him, he cursed himself for getting himself into this impossible situation.

He didn't deserve her quiet understanding. He hadn't had the right to unburden the turmoil of the past months by telling her that story. He wasn't entitled to be here with her at all.

His conscience screamed at him to tell her the truth,

but he couldn't. Not when he'd promised his father he wouldn't reveal their connection.

He should have listened to his father's warning about developing personal relationships with Skillington employees and stayed away from Anna.

It was too late for that now, he thought ruefully. But maybe he could still make things right.

"I owe you an apology for showing up here at the chalet like I did," he said. "Knowing how you felt, I shouldn't have come."

"Apology accepted," she said.

His desire had cooled as he told the story of his parentage, but with her nestled against his side it clearly had taken only a temporary leave of absence.

He hardened his resolve even as he felt his erection grow rigid. He could get through this. He could.

"Tomorrow morning," he said, "once the roads are clear, I'll leave."

She lifted her head from his shoulder. The room was still dark, but his night vision had adjusted and he could read dismay on her face. "But you can't leave."

"Aren't you the same woman who kicked the snow last night because it messed up the roads and trapped me here?" he asked, trying to make a joke of it.

"That was last night," she said. "Things are different now."

"Not so different," he argued. "You're still sharing a bedroom with a man you don't intend to have an affair with."

The feel of her hand on his chest nearly stole his breath. It covered his breastbone, not so very far from his heart, forging an unspoken connection between them.

"At the moment," she said, her breath sweet and warm against his lips, "I'm having a hard time remembering why I said I wouldn't sleep with you."

His body cried out, imploring his mind to forget everything but the feel of her against him. But her comment about desiring to meet his father, the man who signed her paychecks, continued to gnaw at him.

"I remember," he said reluctantly. "You said—"

"Shhh." She placed three fingers against his lips, silencing him. "That's enough talking for tonight."

"But—" he began.

Her lips replaced her fingers, cutting off his half-hearted protest with a kiss so sweet his heart ached.

Those lips, soft and warm, moved over his mouth almost reverently. Tasting. Teasing. And making him feel guilty as hell.

He should stop this before it went any further. She deserved more than a man who could tell her only half truths. No matter that the man wanted her so desperately it had become a gnawing in his gut.

The softness of her silk-clad breasts pressed against his chest, so pleasant he felt pained. The tip of her tongue dipped inside his mouth almost shyly, then withdrew.

He groaned low in his throat, feeling his muscles strain with the effort of holding himself back.

She settled more fully against him and traced his pectoral muscles with the flat of one hand.

His heartbeat sped up, and a little more of his resolve faded.

His hands wanted to roam but he kept them at his sides while he warred with himself. Anna was in his bed and had come willingly into his arms. How was he supposed to resist her? Was it lunacy to even try?

Anna drew slightly back from the temptation of Cole's mouth and put one hand to her head, dismay running through her like a river.

Something wasn't right. She could feel it in the tenseness of Cole's muscles as she caressed him, the hesitancy of his mouth as she kissed him.

Had she misread the signs? Had he changed his mind about making love to her?

"Cole," she asked, trying to keep the growing hurt out of her voice. "Is something wrong?"

"No," he said quickly, shaking his head. His hand came up to stroke her cheek, his fingers lingering at her bottom lip.

"You don't..." Her voice trailed off, but it wasn't her way to not say what was on her mind. "You don't seem too into it."

"Not into it?" He sounded incredulous. "You wouldn't say that if the lights were on."

Even as she felt herself blush, she was tempted to reach out and touch him to verify that he was as turned on as he claimed.

"But then why are you holding back?"

"You wouldn't understand."

"Try me," she said softly.

"Because…" He stopped, started again. "Ah, hell. Because I think I'm falling for you."

It sounded as though the words had slipped out against his will, but Anna didn't care. She smiled while warmth spread through every inch of her body.

"Good," she said smugly and took another taste of his mouth.

This time she didn't sense any resistance. His tongue ran over her lips, nudged against her teeth and slid into the silken heat of her mouth.

She was lying half across him, her upper body plastered against his. He glided a hand over her back, then caressed the rounded flesh of her rear end as his tongue parried with hers.

She'd fantasized about touching him since she'd come across him sitting at his desk with his tie askew on Christmas Eve. Reality was better than the fantasy. He felt solid and strong, like she'd imagined, but she hadn't counted on the low, sexy moans emitting from the back of his throat.

Heat pooled in her stomach, settled in her groin and she felt herself grow damp.

She'd wanted men before, but not like this. Never like this.

One moment, she was on her stomach, lying on top of him. Then the room went topsy-turvy and she was on her back with Cole hovering over her.

Before she could get her bearings, he kissed her with a voracious passion that meshed lips and teeth and tongues. The world spun crazily, robbing her of perspective until only sensation remained.

Finally, he drew back and stripped off his T-shirt. She lifted her arms and, with an impatient motion, he peeled off her nightgown.

"I can't see you," he said in frustration.

Before he could reach toward the lamp, she grabbed his wrist. There was something about the darkness that heightened her sensations, lending their lovemaking an extra dose of intimacy.

"Then feel me," she invited and guided his hand to her breast.

His breathing was uneven as he touched her, hesitantly at first and then more boldly. She felt her breasts swell, her nipples grow taut and a sweet ache develop between her legs. He brought his mouth to one breast while he kneaded the other, and she reveled in the hot, wet feel of his lips and tongue. She arched her back, trying to get closer to him.

With a low growl, he moved his mouth back up to her lips, hauling her against him so that she was where she most wanted to be: Skin to glorious skin.

His was covered by fine, dark hair but underneath felt as smooth as velvet. She couldn't get enough of him, she thought in awe as her hands roamed restlessly over muscles and sinew.

His hands were busy, too, inflaming wherever they touched. She lifted her hips so he could slide off her panties and gasped as he dipped two fingers inside her damp heat. She moaned, moving restlessly against him.

She bit her lip, trying not to climax too soon even as the pressure built inside her. Moving her mouth from his lips to the side of his face, she muttered against his neck, "I want you naked, too."

"Your wish is my command."

He probably meant it as a quip but the sentence came out as a strangled cry. Laughing at himself a little, he made short work of his underwear.

She started to pull him back into her arms when she remembered something that should have occurred to her before she'd started any of this.

"Condom?" she asked hopefully.

He was off the bed so quick, she didn't have time to worry. His bag must have been next to the bed because she heard the whir of a zipper and then the rustle of foil packages.

He tossed the extras onto the nightstand, tore open one of the packages and was back by her side within seconds.

"I see you came prepared," she said as he sheathed himself.

He stopped in the action of covering himself. It was easier to see his expression now that her eyes had adjusted to the darkness but impossible to read the nuances in them.

"Does that bother you?" he asked.

It might have a few hours ago, but that was before he'd shared that intimate part of himself with her in the darkness. Not his body, but his mind.

Her hand joined his, circling his erect length. He gasped as she helped him finish the job of putting on the condom.

"I'm only glad one of us came prepared."

"Ah, Anna," he said when he was lying next to her and she was once more in his arms, "I should ask you again if you're sure, but I'm not going to."

She smiled against his lips.

"I'll answer anyway," she said. "I'm sure."

Speaking what was in her heart seemed to free her inhibitions and she positioned herself against his arousal, rubbing against him so he could have no doubt what she wanted.

"I don't want to wait," she said as she opened her legs and guided him to the heart of her.

He was on his elbows, for some reason trying not to thrust into her in one fluid stroke as her body cried out for him to do. She lifted her hips, impaling herself with him.

Their groans sounded in tandem.

"Oh, Cole," she said in the instant before he started to move. "Didn't know anything could feel...so...good."

Their rhythms matched, she thought dimly as they moved together, as if they were two parts of a whole. He kissed her as the tension built and she kissed him back, thrusting her tongue into his mouth the same way he was thrusting inside of her.

She'd had sex before, experiences she'd found pleasing more often than not. But something was different this time despite the customary bedroom setting and unimaginative positioning of their bodies.

Not only different, but extraordinary. Her breathing came quicker, her heart beat faster, the tension ran higher.

In a flash, she knew why: because this time she was making love with Cole.

She felt herself cresting toward the elusive place where sensation reigned, but then he stopped moving.

"No, no," she begged. "Don't stop."

She looked into his face and could see that his eyes were shut. "Want to make...good...for you," he said, the words an obvious strain.

"It's already better than good," she said, lifting against him in invitation. He groaned once, then pumped into her, and she came apart.

Fireworks seemed to detonate inside her, rushing upward, brightening her world like they lightened the sky. She moaned against his mouth at the intensity of it all as they roiled through her, in wave after wave of brilliant color.

He thrust into her again, setting off another array of feeling as he cried out. His body spasmed in time with hers until, finally, at long last, they lay still and replete in each other's arms.

It seemed like hours, but might only have been moments, before their heartbeats slowed and their breathing returned to something resembling normalcy.

Only then did she realize that her arms were thrown over her head and he was holding both her hands.

I'm falling for you, too, Cole Mansfield, she thought, shocked that she felt the words clean through to the center of her heart.

That was a problem. She knew that. But at the moment, she didn't have the desire or the energy to figure out why.

He squeezed her hands, kissed her softly on the lips and rolled to the side so he was no longer on top of her.

"No," she protested when he pulled out of her.

He sat up, took care of the condom, then turned back to her. "What do you mean no?" he asked, and she saw the white flash of his teeth in the darkness.

"I wasn't ready for you to—" She paused, then said with asperity, "You know what I meant by no."

He laughed, a joyous sound that rumbled through her like happiness, then pulled another silver packet from the bedside table.

"Honey," he said, turning back to her, "I'm not going anywhere."

"Good," she said.

And the best sex Anna had ever had in her life proceeded to get even better.

8

A MAN'S HAND WAS on her thigh, gliding over the naked skin of her hip and venturing higher.

Anna sighed in pleasure as the large, warm hand leisurely traced the indentation of her waist and ventured over her rib cage before reaching her breast.

"Mmmmm," she said as her breast grew full and heavy. A liquid sensation filled her.

She'd had erotic dreams of Cole before, but this one was starting out to be the best one yet.

"Wake up, sleeping beauty."

She loved the deep, sexy rumble of his voice. She shut her eyes tighter, clinging to sleep, reluctant to leave such a lovely dreamland. But still she knew the drill.

"Doesn't wake up without a kiss," she murmured, and the lover of her dreams laughed.

He kissed like a man who had been created from her secret desires should. His lips were firm yet soft, knowledgeable about how to coax a response from her.

She loved kissing him, loved the hot, wet sensation of his mouth on hers. She tangled her hands in his thick hair, not wanting to let him go, her eyes still shut. Despite what she'd said, she didn't want to wake up.

The pealing of a phone interrupted her lovely dream.

Something wasn't quite right. This was her dream,

her fantasy. She wasn't especially fond of phones so it seemed unlikely that she would insert one in her dream. She especially wouldn't put one in this part.

Even as the Cole of her dreams continued to kiss her, the phone kept ringing.

Darn. She was going to have to wake up.

She pursed her lips in disappointment, ending the dreamy kiss, and opened her eyes.

The sunlight filtering through the miniblinds was glaringly bright. It hurt her eyes and threw the room, so dark the night before, into focus.

Cole's face was inches from hers, his dark eyes soft, his lower jaw darkened with a day's worth of whiskers, his hair mussed from sleep. His lips were moist, as though from kisses.

"Good morning," he said.

His well-defined, hair-sprinkled chest was bare. A sheet was bunched so far below his waist that his naked hip was visible. Underneath the covers, she was as naked as he was.

The events of the night before rushed back to her and closed around her mind like a fist.

This morning's up-close-and-personal interlude with Cole hadn't been a dream. It was a continuation of the night before when she'd practically insisted he make love to her.

He'd obliged her. Over and over again.

Her eyes dipped. By the look of things, he was primed to accommodate her again.

The phone still rang, but he paid it no mind. He slid a thumb over her cheek and across her lips before cupping the back of her head. The gentle pressure he exerted invited her to move closer.

She resisted the pressure, torn between wanting him and knowing she should consider the wisdom of what was happening between them.

Last night, when her defenses had been down, she'd given in to overwhelming desire. But at the corners of her mind, she seemed to remember she had a reason for not wanting to get involved with him. A very good reason. One of his hands moved across her hip in a sensual caress. If only she could remember what it was.

"Anna?" He said her name like a question. She barely heard him over the persistent ringing of the phone.

She saw in his eyes that he was confused about why she hesitated this late in the game. She was baffled herself, especially because she longed to damn the consequences and spend the rest of the morning making love. His hand moved to her breast, and whatever will she had to resist him started to fade.

She sighed, ready to capitulate, when the phone rang again. Like a warning bell.

"We should answer that," she said over what must have been the ninth or tenth ring.

"Somebody else will get it," Cole said, his eyes half-lidded, his mouth advancing.

Anna turned her head from what she wanted, and his kiss landed on her cheek. She shivered at the sensation of his mouth on her skin and tried to focus on the alarm clock. It showed the shockingly late hour of ten o'clock.

"Surely the others in the house are awake by now," Anna said. "Why haven't they answered?"

"I don't know." Frustration thickened his voice. "Maybe for the same reason we're not answering."

"We need to get it," Anna said.

"The answering machine can get it."

"This house doesn't have an answering machine," she said amid the chiming. "And the phone call must be important or the caller would have hung up already."

With a low growl and a quick motion, he stretched out one long arm and snatched the phone from its cradle on the bedside table nearest him.

"Hello," he all but barked into the receiver.

The harsh lines of his face relaxed as he listened to the caller, but only slightly.

"Yes, we're still in bed." Pause. "No, we were already awake." Another pause. "A wonderful time, thank you." Yet another. "Yes, she is here."

He handed the receiver to her. "It's for you."

She half sat up in bed and arranged the covers the best she could around her nakedness. He quirked a brow at her.

"Who is it?" she mouthed as she took the receiver.

"Your mother," he said.

She nearly dropped the phone.

He'd told *her mother* they were in bed together? Not in those words exactly but close enough that Rosemary Wesley couldn't possibly have missed the implication.

"Anna? Are you there?" Her mother's high-octane voice came over the phone line loud and clear. Why hadn't Anna heard it a moment ago when it wasn't too late to warn Cole to be circumspect?

"Yes, Mom," she said into the receiver. "I'm here."

"Cole tells me you two are having a wonderful time," her mother said expansively.

Anna narrowed her eyes and shot daggers at Cole, who held up his hands in a "What did I do?" pose. As if he hadn't foreseen what kinds of conclusions Rosemary Wesley would reach when he'd confirmed he was in bed with her daughter.

"It's been okay," Anna said.

She would not, under any circumstances, tell her mother that Cole was a wonderful lover. Even though he had been.

"If you're still in bed at ten o'clock, things are better than okay," her mother said bluntly, "but you shouldn't be talking to your mother about things like that."

Anna closed her eyes in mortification. Her mother would never believe she and Cole weren't involved now. The older woman was so notorious for her lack of discretion that nobody else in Anna's family would ever believe it, either.

"Why are you calling, Mother?" Anna asked.

"I want to know what's going on up there."

Cole was leaning against the sleigh bed's headboard with both arms behind his neck, resembling a muscle-bound centerfold. He watched her through half-lidded eyes. Bedroom eyes. One of them winked at her.

"Isn't it obvious?" she hissed at her mother.

"No, it is not obvious. I'm at your aunt's house. I came over here this morning to water Miranda's plants. Not five minutes later, she comes through the door."

"Aunt Miranda's there?" Anna asked.

Cole sat up straighter. "Your aunt's in Pittsburgh?"

"She's here and she's not talking," her mother said. "You know what a drama queen she can be. All she told me is that she and Peter had a fight. Is he there?"

"I don't know," Anna said helplessly. Cole was sitting up without the support of the headboard now. He shrugged and held up his hands. Obviously he could hear her mother's end of the conversation.

"Well, go check and call me back at Miranda's," her mother said. "This is bad, Anna. I think she might leave him."

"Do you want me to check on your uncle?" Cole asked when she hung up the phone.

The offer was tempting, but Anna couldn't accept it. Not when Cole was already far too involved in her family's business.

"No, thanks. I'll do it," she said.

She got out of bed, taking the top sheet with her. She wrapped herself toga style, the way movie stars sometimes did in films without an R-rating, and scrounged around for some clothes.

"Any particular reason you don't want me to see you naked?" Cole asked.

He was still on the bed, the remaining sheets offering him scant coverage. He looked like that sculpture of The Thinker, only in the flesh and blood.

She hastily pulled some clothes out of a dresser she'd stuffed the day before. She avoided his eyes as she hurried to the bathroom.

"None I want to talk about," she said, shutting his

question out of her mind. She didn't want to think about it, either.

She came out of the bathroom in black leggings and a thick blue sweater a few minutes later, finger-combing hair she hadn't taken time to brush. She'd focused her mental energy on Miranda and Peter's problem, partly because she didn't want to think about her own.

"We'll have to talk about this nudity aversion you have sometime," her problem called from the bed, picking up the conversation where they'd left off.

She pursed her lips. He made her sound like a prude, which he had to know wasn't true after last night. "I'm not averse to getting nude."

"Me, neither," he said.

Wasn't that the truth, she thought as she walked to the door. She didn't look at him because she was human and therefore as susceptible to a gorgeous, naked male in her bed as the next woman.

Clothes. She needed him to put on clothes.

"You take the shower first," she called on her way out of the room. "I might be a while."

She shut the sight of Cole in her bed out of her mind and went in search of her uncle. She found him in the corner of the chalet's great room at the same desk he'd occupied for most of the trip.

He was showered and dressed, his beard neatly combed as though he'd been awake for hours. He tapped the end of his pen on his teeth as he stared into his laptop.

"Uncle Peter?"

He glanced up at her as she entered the room.

"You're awake," he said. "I was starting to think you and Cole would sleep the day away. Where is he anyway?"

"Showering," Anna answered a second before she realized how intimate the answer sounded. She needed to change the subject. "Uncle Peter, did you know that Aunt—"

"That's one bright fellow, your Cole," he interrupted, leaning back in his seat. "We talked some last night, and he has a good head for business. What did you say he did at Skillington?"

Anna set her lips, refraining from correcting his misconception that Cole was hers. The sooner she answered his question, the sooner she could figure out what was going on between her aunt and him.

"He's my assistant," she said shortly.

"A man like that an assistant? Really?" Uncle Peter drew out the syllable, then shook his head. "He won't be an assistant for long." He winked at her. "If I were you, Anna, I'd watch out for my job."

Anna blinked as his comment registered, aware that it was eerily similar to what she'd been telling herself since she hired Cole. She felt as though she'd been blind and now she could see.

That's what had been nagging at the back of her mind this morning when Cole had been kissing her. He was the man who wanted her job.

"So what did you come downstairs to tell me?" Uncle Peter continued, oblivious to her distress. "I'd wager it's about the phone call."

Anna forced her mind back to Uncle Peter and his

predicament. That's why she'd come downstairs, not to have the sense knocked back into her about Cole.

"It was my mother calling from your house to say that Aunt Miranda's there." At his impassive impression, she continued, "You don't seem surprised."

"I'm not," he said dryly. "Miranda came downstairs at about seven-thirty this morning and said she was leaving."

"And you didn't try to stop her?"

"When your aunt gets something in her mind, it doesn't do any good to talk to her," he said, a trace of bitterness in his voice. He glanced pointedly down at his laptop. "Is that it? Because I have work to do."

Rendered speechless both by his response and his comments about Cole, Anna tramped up the hardwood stairs to the second floor of the chalet. Her hand gripped the banister so tightly her knuckles turned white.

She was partially inside the bedroom she shared with Cole when the heavy oak door next to it opened. Julie and Drew emerged, their arms draped around each other.

"Morning, Anna. Did I hear a phone ringing a little while ago?" Julie cast her husband a happy glance. "Drew and I were in the shower."

Envy rose in Anna even as she fought against it. She shouldn't want to shower with Cole, not when the obstacle of their jobs stood between them.

"Anna, is something wrong?" her sister asked.

"Yes," Anna answered but quickly realized she couldn't hash out the problem she had with Cole here in the hall. "It's...Aunt Miranda. Mom called a little while ago to say she was back in Pittsburgh."

Julie gave a dramatic gasp and covered her mouth while Anna told them about her conversation with Uncle Peter. They were discussing how they could help put the fractured marriage back together when Anna heard the creak of a door opening.

The newlyweds must have heard it, too, because they gazed past her into the bedroom.

Cole emerged from the bathroom toweling his thick dark hair. He'd shaved and wore only a pair of jeans unsnapped at the waist. Behind him, the bed was unmade. The sheets were in a rumpled tangle, as though they'd somehow been in the way.

Cole gave them all a half wave and a little smile. Julie's eyes did a wicked dance when she turned them to Anna.

"It's too bad about Uncle Peter and Aunt Miranda, but looks like the trip isn't going poorly for everyone."

"It's not what you think," Anna began, but Julie's grin only broadened.

Anna followed the path of her sister's eyes to the brief silk nightgown and even briefer panties that she'd neglected to pick up that morning. They were lying in a careless tangle not far from the bed.

"I think it is what I think," Julie whispered to her. "All I can say is bully for you."

Julie kissed her on the cheek, as though congratulations were in order because she'd slept with Cole. Her employee. The man who wanted her job.

"We can talk about Aunt Miranda and Uncle Peter

later," Julie said in a louder voice. She took Drew by the hand, leading him away from the doorway.

"Wait," Anna said, but the couple continued walking down the hallway believing that she and Cole were together. She pulled the door shut and leaned against it. How could this have happened?

"Peter still here?" Cole asked as he rummaged in his bag.

"Yep," she said. "It doesn't look like he plans to go anywhere soon, either."

He glanced up from what he was doing. "You sound angry."

"I am angry."

"Look, I know it's hard to see your aunt and uncle having problems, but the best thing for you to do is to stay out of it."

"Why?" she said, throwing up her hands and stalking to his side. "Nobody stays out of *my* business. Thanks to you, everybody in my family is even more sure we're involved."

"We slept together, Anna," he said in a calm voice that infuriated her even more.

"That doesn't mean everybody has to know about it."

"I didn't tell them."

"You answered the phone," she said. "You came out of the bathroom half-naked."

"I didn't take a shirt into the bathroom," he said in what she refused to consider was a reasonable answer. "I didn't know you'd be standing there with the door to the hall wide open."

"So now it's my fault?"

"What are you talking about?"

"The way my family is pushing us together."

"Us sleeping together had nothing to do with your family."

"You're crazy if you believe that. Miranda was the one who arranged for us to have a room with only the one bed."

"We're the ones who decided to make love."

"No, no," she said, shaking her head. "You're muddling the issue. Just because they're pushing me toward you doesn't mean I'll go. I haven't forgotten you're still that guy who wants my job."

"I thought we were past the job thing."

"The job is who I am," she said, then shook her head. "I can't deal with this right now. I can't deal with you."

"Fine," he said. He pulled on a shirt, socks and shoes. "Looks to me like you need to calm down before you can deal with anyone."

"Is that right?"

"Yeah, that's right," he said with a stony stare when he was dressed. "We can talk about this later when you're more reasonable. I'm going out."

"Go," she shot back, wincing a little when the door closed with a resounding bang.

She sank down onto the unmade bed and covered her face with her hands. She wanted to call him back, if only to make sure he didn't do something foolish, like try to ski.

But she didn't.

Because she was terribly afraid that the more time she

spent with him in the bedroom, the less likely she'd be to remember why she shouldn't mix business and pleasure.

COLE TRUDGED THROUGH the snow in his heavy boots, pulling behind him a long red cord attached to an inflated black tube. The rubber tube resembled an oversized tire, without the grooves and with a smooth underside that completely covered one side of the thing.

He paused, surveying the tubing hill before him.

Four rope tows pulled snow tubes full of laughing, smiling people up the mountain to the raucous strains of pop music.

Snaking down the mountain were twelve tubing runs, complete with twists, bumps and miniature walls of snow built on either side of them to prevent lane changing.

Fully seventy-five percent of the few hundred people on the hill were children.

Great, Cole thought sarcastically as he sniffled and braced himself against a particularly stiff wind.

Not only had one of the worst mornings of his life followed closely on the heels of his best-ever night, but it was soon to be chased by a hideous afternoon.

He could tell by a mere glance at the tubing hill—and the fact that his fingers felt frozen inside his gloves—that it wasn't his scene.

His preferred mode of transportation was a sleek, swift bicycle. His chosen setting, a warm, sunny day.

But he might as well at least try to make the best of it while he gave Anna a chance to cool down.

He understood that working together was a problem for her. Hell, considering the secret he was keeping from her, it was a quandary for him. But he'd thought they got past that last night. He'd thought they had connected on a level that had nothing to do with work.

He dragged the tube behind him in the packed snow until he got to the rope tow. He waited his turn, feeling as though he was going to visit the executioner.

"Hey, mister, you gonna stand there all day?"

The comment came from a gum-chewing rope tow operator, who looked about seventeen. His job was to loop the end of the cord onto a heavy plastic hook that carried the tube up the mountain.

"Butt in the hole," the teen ordered, gesturing at the tube.

Cole plopped onto the tube, only to be jerked up the hill by the lift.

"You sit down that hard next time, you'll deflate the thing," the teen yelled after him.

Everybody stared. The young girl getting on the rope lift after him giggled.

Cole had doubts about whether the rope could hold all of his two hundred thirty pounds but found himself slowly creeping up the mountain.

This wasn't so bad, Cole thought as he took in the snow-covered pine trees and the clear blue sky. It was even sort of pleasurable, if you didn't count the extreme cold.

Maybe it was an omen that things would ultimately work out between Anna and him.

Sure, it hadn't been a good sign that she was loath for

her family to think they were involved. And there was the not-so-small matter of her not knowing Arthur Skillington was his father. Not to mention that she'd acted like she never wanted to see him again.

But with the sun shining and the hill alive with laughter, their problems didn't seem insurmountable.

He was so lost in thought that the small hill at the end of the rope tow's run took him by surprise.

His cord disengaged from the yellow plastic hook that had been pulling his tube up the mountain, and his tube went skidding down a miniature hill.

He sat there in his tube for a few moments, stunned by the suddenness in which the ride had ended.

It was a couple of moments too long.

The tube in which the giggling girl behind him was sitting crashed into his. She bounced off him like a bowling pin.

"You're supposed to move your tube out of the way before anyone else comes, mister," the girl said crossly, no longer giggling.

"Sorry," he said, but she was already stalking away from him.

He unfolded his long length from the tube seconds before another rider slammed into it. This time only the tube went flying.

"What's your problem?" a gap-toothed kid asked as Cole went to retrieve his abused tube.

He hoped he'd been wrong about the ride on the rope tow being an omen.

The way his day was going, it could only be a bad one.

ANNA STOOD NEAR the bottom of the tubing hill behind a fence separating tubers from spectators. She shielded her eyes from the sun with one hand while she tried to find Cole.

It shouldn't be too hard. The median age on the hill appeared to be about twelve, which should make Cole stand out like Gulliver in the land of the Lilliputians.

The difficult part would be knowing what to say when she did locate him.

She'd come to the tubing hill without a plan, equipped only with the knowledge that it wasn't her way to run away from her problems.

One thing was certain: Cole Mansfield had become a problem.

She'd told him as much during her tirade that morning, but she'd also stated that she couldn't deal with him right then. That had been wrong. She always tackled her problems as they came.

"Oh, my gosh, look at that awesome chain." A young boy paused in the act of pulling his snow tube toward a rope tow and pointed up the mountain.

Anna took a casual glance in the direction the boy indicated.

A chain of seven snow tubes shot down the mountain at a speed easily twice as fast as single riders traveled on adjacent runs. The six trailing tubers held onto the tubes in front of them for what looked like dear life. They were obviously children.

Nobody would mistake the lead tuber for a child. Even from a distance, he was massive. His arms and legs stuck out from the tube at haphazard angles as the seven-tube chain skidded down the run at top speed.

"Cole," Anna said aloud.

She barely heard herself, so loud were the delighted screams of the children as the chain covered the last third of the mountain.

Cole's teeth flashed, as white as the snow he traveled over. He let out a deep-throated yell as he passed the point where she stood, then dug his heels in the snow to slow down the chain's momentum.

The seven tubes finally came to a sliding halt a good distance farther down the hill than most of the other tubers.

Cole rose from the tube and the children followed suit. He looked like the Pied Piper of White Tower.

"Again, again," the children clamored.

They were all boys, probably in the vicinity of eight or nine years old. All six of them wore identical knit hats, royal-blue with some sort of insignia on the front.

"Again?" Cole laughed. "How many times did that one make it?"

"Not enough," one of the boys cried. "Never enough."

Another took his hand and dragged him in the direction of the rope tow. "Hurry up, Cole. It's almost time for us to leave."

"All right, all right," Cole said grudgingly, but Anna saw through him and knew he wasn't truly reluctant.

The group had to pass by her to get to the nearest rope tow and did so with gusto, whooping in anticipation of another wild run.

The smallest boy lagged behind. Cole stopped, gave the boy a good-natured pat on the back and stacked his tube on top of his own. He headed toward the tow with double the burden as before, and something caught in Anna's chest.

He looked up then, his professor glasses so frosted over with snow that she wasn't sure until he spoke whether he saw her.

"Anna," he said and stopped. A boy behind him careened into him. "What are you doing here?"

"Uncle Peter told me where you were," she answered.

She might have given him the longer answer if the kids hadn't been impatiently dancing around him: After returning her mother's call and taking a long shower, she'd concluded that she'd acted like a coward.

"Come on, Cole," a boy with a nose as bright as his red mittens urged.

Now that the boys were closer, the image inside the yellow and dark-blue design on their hats was clear. It was a wolf cub. The boys, then, were Cub Scouts.

"You think you guys can go without me?" Cole asked, taking off his glasses and cleaning them.

"No way. We wouldn't go nearly as fast," cried a pale boy with white-blond eyebrows that matched the tufts of hair sticking out of his hat.

"Maybe you can find another sucker...I mean, tuber...to ride with you."

"Nobody else is as good as you," cried a chubby boy in a bright yellow jacket.

"Yeah," said a child who looked skinny despite all

his winter gear. "You're the biggest man on the mountain."

"I make them go faster," Cole explained as an aside to Anna. "Their troop leader's a little guy. They adopted me about an hour ago."

"Hey, you're pretty big, too," the skinny boy told Anna. "Why don't you come be on our chain?"

She lifted an eyebrow at Cole. "Thanks," she told the boy. "I think."

"Come on before you get mobbed." Cole grabbed a tube from a nearby stack and piled it on top of his and the little boy's. Then he took her gloved hand in his. "These kids don't take no for an answer."

Anna had learned to ski when she was in grade school, well before the snow tubing craze had made its mark on the nation's ski resorts.

"Would you believe I've never done this before," she told Cole at the top of the run.

"There isn't much to it," Cole said. "The kids always make me go first because I'm biggest. You'll have to be second. Just hold on to my tube."

"It's our turn!" the kid in the yellow jacket yelled.

Laughing at their enthusiasm, Anna sat down in her tube. The child directly behind her grabbed onto it.

"Let's go," a couple of the kids yelled in unison.

They pushed into the packed snow on top of the hill with their heels, slowly inching forward until Cole's tube began sliding down the hill.

The rest of them followed, like the sections of a giant caterpillar, picking up speed amazingly quickly.

Flakes of blowing snow hit Anna full in the face along

with the force of the wind. Her stomach leaped into her throat.

The six children behind them screamed. Anna did, too. Her eyes watered but she wasn't sure whether it was from delight or the wind.

Almost as soon as it began, the ride ended. She dug her heels into the snow to help Cole stop their momentum, and the tubes behind them came to a jarring stop.

She stood up, feeling as though she'd left her stomach in the tube. Her legs wobbled.

"That was way cool," she told Cole.

He got out of his tube much more slowly. Under his tan, his face was white.

"Yeah," he said before affixing a grin but she'd seen enough to know it was false.

"Cole Mansfield," she said under her breath so only he could hear, "why are you doing this if you're not enjoying yourself?"

He shrugged, then indicated the laughing, dancing children. "For them," he said.

Her heart melted faster than snow during a heat wave.

She'd been angry at him for something when she came to the tubing area, but for the life of her she couldn't remember what.

But whatever it was, it no longer seemed the slightest bit important.

9

COLE SETTLED HIS ARM more snugly around Anna as their horse-drawn sleigh hit a rough patch on the snow-covered path.

She tipped up her head, slanted him a grateful smile and gave him a swift, soft kiss that was full of promise.

That pretty much settled it, Cole thought in wonder. He would never understand women.

He had only a vague notion of why she'd blasted him this morning after that incredible night of lovemaking. He had an even dimmer idea of the reason for her about-face.

A gloved hand tapped him on the shoulder. He and Anna both turned to regard her sister Julie, who sat next to Drew in the back seat of their four-rider sleigh.

It had been so quiet back there for most of the trip that Cole doubted the newlyweds had paid much attention to the majesty of the snow-capped trees and sloping, white hills.

"Isn't this fun?" Julie's cheeks were so rosy, she looked like a cherub. Her lips were even redder, but Cole doubted it was from the cold. "I'm so glad you two let me talk you into coming along."

"Me, too," Anna said, giving Cole's arm a squeeze. At least he thought it was a squeeze. The layers of clothes he wore to ward off the chill of a wintry Pennsylvania night made it hard to tell.

"I'm glad, too," Cole said, surprised it was true.

A frigid ride through the mountains wasn't his idea of the ideal way to make up. The lining of his lungs felt frozen from breathing in the crisp, cold air. The snow that drifted down from the sky in delicate white flakes were bothersome enough that he'd had to remove his glasses.

The arm he had around Anna was propped up on layers of down. Even if he'd been able to touch her exposed skin, it wouldn't have done much good. Despite his gloves, the feeling in his fingers was all but gone.

But Anna was happy, and that was enough for Cole.

"I can't believe the ride's ending so soon," Anna said as the stable came into view and the two draft horses pulling the sleigh picked up the pace.

Cole couldn't believe it had taken so long. Even the horses, a sturdy breed covered with thick coats of hair, seemed to have had enough. They wouldn't be running hell-bent for the stables if they hadn't.

He hoped for the horses' sake that the stables, like the chalet, boasted one of man's greatest inventions: central heat.

He didn't start to warm up until they were in the foyer. Even then, he debated the wisdom of taking off his coat before the thaw was thoroughly underway.

Julie made the decision for him, grabbing him by his still-jacketed arm and pulling him into the kitchen.

"It looks to me like everything's going according to

plan," she said in a stage whisper when they were alone beside the microwave. "Am I right?"

He thought briefly about sticking his hands in the microwave to warm them but rubbed them together instead.

"Everything's going fine," he said slowly.

"I thought so." Julie's red-brown hair bounced as she nodded happily. Her freckles stood out starkly against her luminous skin. "I've been trying to do what I can. But of course, Anna being Anna, there's not a whole lot I can do."

"Anna is Anna," Cole said, mostly because she seemed to expect a response.

"She hasn't had the best luck with men but I can tell the tide has turned. Just remember," she said and winked at him, "I'm on your side."

"Julie," he said, bending his head down in conspirator fashion, "what are we talking about?"

Her eyes widened. "Your plan." When he didn't reply, she punched him lightly on the shoulder. "To win over Anna. Don't tell me you didn't know I knew."

"Knew what?"

"That you're not really Anna's boyfriend."

Cole felt his lower jaw drop. "If you knew I wasn't her boyfriend, why did you invite me along on this ski trip?"

She pursed her lips, seeming to think about that. "Anna hasn't had real good luck with men in the past, but you're different. You're exactly what she needs."

"And what's that?"

"A man who tells it like it is," she said. "Not to mention being so nuts about her that he'll put up with my family."

He gave her a wry smile and not only because her assessment of his integrity was off. "I like your family. I like Anna, too. But I'm not so sure I've won her over."

"That's why I'm making sure Drew doesn't get out of the bedroom tonight." Her eyebrows danced. "The hot tub's all yours. There's a bottle of Anna's favorite Beaujolais in the wine rack. That might help, too."

She gave him a sunny smile, then kissed him lightly on the cheek. "Good luck," she said before practically skipping away.

When Cole was alone, he finally took off his jacket. A miraculous warmth spread through him, no doubt due to the fantasy of what he'd like to do to Anna in the hot tub.

Judging by the way she'd acted on the sleigh ride, he could probably act out his fantasy. But he wanted more than a single night of hot bliss, which is what he'd get if he and Anna didn't settle a few things before they indulged themselves with each other.

He couldn't tell her he was Arthur Skillington's son, but he could make her understand she already mattered more to him than a job.

ANNA SIPPED HER BEAUJOLAIS while she watched Cole lift fresh lumber from the log rack on the hearth and pile it into the fireplace.

After they'd returned from the sleigh ride, she'd fully expected him to suggest they retreat directly to the bedroom. She couldn't decide whether she was annoyed or relieved that he hadn't.

Her feelings were so jumbled where he was concerned, she wasn't sure of anything at all.

"Good night, Anna. Good night, Cole," her sister Julie called from the foot of the stairs. She yawned hugely. "Drew and I are super tired. We're going straight to bed. There's no way we're leaving the room until morning."

"Sleep well, then," Anna said even as she wondered at her sister's bright eyes and cheery smile. She didn't look weary. Energy radiated off her, as though an all-night ski marathon wouldn't be out of the question.

"Good night," Cole called.

Before Julie left the room, she winked at him. Anna whipped her head around to register Cole's reaction, but his face was impassive as he lit the fire with a long-stemmed match.

He poked at the logs with a tool from the ornate brass set next to the fireplace until the logs crackled and smoke gently rose up the chimney. Firelight danced over his face, infusing his skin with reds and oranges, making him appear even more of a hottie.

He straightened and she imagined his sleek muscles rippling under his clothes. He moved toward her with a pantherlike grace, and she braced herself for the familiar rush of awareness that resulted from contact with his body. But he sat down a good twelve inches from her on the sofa.

That abruptly decided the annoyed-or-relieved debate for Anna. First the fire, now the distance. Didn't the man remember they'd made love the night before? And what had Julie's wink been about?

"I wonder where your uncle Peter is," he said before she could ask either question. Now that Drew and Julie were upstairs, the chalet was quiet aside from the crackling fire, the whir of the heater and the ticking of a grandfather clock. "He's been going over to the lodge at night but he's usually back by now."

"I must've forgotten to tell you," Anna said unhappily. This was not what she wanted to talk about. "Uncle Peter hitched a ride with a business associate he ran into. He left this afternoon."

"Maybe he means to patch things up with your aunt."

"I don't think so." Julie shook her head. "He said work had piled up and he needed to spend the next couple days in the office."

Cole set his wineglass down on the polished wood of the coffee table and looked deeply into her eyes. "He's a fool if he puts his work before his woman."

Anna stiffened, jerked back to reality by his comment. She hadn't expected him to reintroduce the subject of work, not when she'd conveniently shoved it to the back of her mind. It reminded her that they weren't simply a man and a woman enjoying a fire. They were rivals for a job.

"Work's important," she stated.

"I never said it wasn't. My point is that other things in life are more important."

She ran a hand over her forehead. "You don't understand."

He crossed his arms over his broad chest. "You're right. I don't. Why don't you explain it to me."

She hesitated, wondering how best to convey what her job meant to her. An image from the past flashed into her mind of she and her grandmother in the kitchen baking chocolate-chip cookies, of the door opening...

"My Grandpa Ziemanski was a coal miner," she said, seeing him in her mind's eye walk slowly, laboriously into the kitchen. "One day when I was about thirteen, I gave him a freshly baked cookie. He took a bite but he was coughing so hard from the coal particles he'd breathed that day he couldn't finish it.

"His back was stooped and I knew it was from hard labor. You know Grandpa. He didn't complain. But I could tell his job was drudgery. I'll always remember what he said when I asked why he didn't quit."

She grew silent, remembering the resignation that had come over her grandfather's face.

"What did he say?" Cole prompted.

"He told me that only a lucky few love their jobs. The rest endure because they have no choice. If work was fun, he said, it wouldn't be called work."

Cole picked up his wine, watching her over the rim of the glass as he drank from it. "You made up your mind to be one of the lucky ones?"

She nodded. "The problem was that I didn't know what I wanted to do. I was creative and good with a computer so I sort of fell into marketing. My first job was with a company that sold office equipment. I worked there a year before I admitted it was as much of a drudge to me as coal mining had been to my grandfather."

His brows drew together. "You don't seem to find marketing drudgery any longer."

"That's because I discovered the secret to loving my job was loving what I was marketing. Winter's my favorite season and I adore winter sports, especially skiing. So Skillington's a perfect fit for me."

"So that's why the job's so important to you?"

"That's right," she said while the doubts about getting further involved with him swam anew in her head. "I'm not looking for greener pastures. From where I stand, my pasture is plenty green enough."

Cole put down his wineglass and tucked a strand of hair behind her ear. Just like that, the sexual awareness between them was back. The air in the room seemed to thicken, the perception as tangible as the smoke swirling up the fireplace.

"Why can't you share the pasture with me?" he asked.

She turned her head and his hand fell away. This wasn't a safe subject, not when she couldn't trust him not to snatch her job from under her. She cast about for something else they could talk about.

"Why did Julie wink at you?" she asked.

"I hadn't realized we were talking about Julie."

"We are now," Anna said, "and I want to know why she winked at you."

When he turned his gaze to the fire, Anna wasn't sure if it was because he had something to hide or whether he was frustrated that she'd changed the subject.

"How can you be sure it was a wink?" he finally asked. "Maybe she had something in her eye."

"Nice try, but I'm not buying it," Anna said, more sure by the second that there was something to uncover. "So why did she wink at you? Was it because of what she was telling you in the kitchen?"

She heard him release a breath.

"I'll worm it out of you eventually so you might as well tell me now and get it over with," she pressed.

"Okay. You win." He turned the full power of his gaze on her. His blue eyes seemed hot, as though warmed by the fire. "She thinks I should try my luck with you in the hot tub tonight."

"I can't believe this," Anna cried. She leaped to her feet, paced to the fireplace and back to the sofa. "No, I take that back. Yes, I do believe it. Julie's just like the rest of my family. Always trying to tell me what to do."

Cole put his hands behind his neck and leaned back against the sofa cushion, watching her carefully. "So you don't want to make love in the hot tub?"

She stopped pacing and thought of Cole's body sliding against hers the night before, of the sensual bliss of having him inside her.

"That's not the issue," she said. "The issue is that I'm not going to."

"Why not?" he asked as though it were a perfectly logical question. Didn't he understand what was happening here?

"Because my sister wants me to."

"That's a convenient excuse," he said.

She narrowed her eyes. "I don't understand what you're getting at."

"Don't think I can't see what you're doing, Anna. You're afraid to get too close to me so you use your family as an excuse to keep me at a distance."

"That doesn't make sense."

"Sure it does. You did it this morning, too. You don't want to admit you're falling for me so you try to convince yourself that your family is pushing us together."

"My family *is* pushing us together."

He unhooked the fingers he had laced behind his neck and straightened his spine, his hands dangling between them. His dark gaze was so intent she felt as though he was seeing through her.

"I have a theory about that," he said. "You're too strong and independent for your family to make you do anything you don't want."

"Meaning?"

"Meaning you made love with me last night because you wanted to, not because they wanted you to."

She hadn't realized she was standing so close to him until his hand shot out and captured hers. He tugged, causing her to lose her balance so that she fell into his lap.

"Know what else I think?" he asked, his mouth inches from her lips.

"What?" She tried to sound angry but was afraid she just sounded breathless. Her bottom nestled against the solid thickness of his thighs and her chest was millimeters from the full-body contact she'd craved earlier that evening.

"The only reason you're going to kiss me right now is because you want to."

"I'm not going to kiss—"

A large hand at her back yanked her to him so that her breasts came flush against his rock-hard chest. Excitement shuddered through her. Her eyes fastened on his mouth. His lips were slightly apart and so beautifully shaped she had an urge to trace the masculine curve with her fingertips.

She tried to quash it, but her hand rose and followed the path of his mouth. She lifted her eyes, met the banked passion in his and knew she was lost.

He was right. She was going to kiss him.

The passion that had started to simmer between them on Christmas Eve flared to life, exactly as it had the night before in the king-sized bed. Her heart pounded and a honeyed heat pooled deep inside her.

He was right about something else, too.

Kissing him had nothing to do with her family. Neither had bringing him home for dinner, enjoying his company at Christmas or agreeing to have him along on the ski vacation.

Kissing him had only to do with wanting him.

With a little moan, she surrendered to the inevitable and kissed him. Passion flared, sizzling and unrelenting. She deepened the kiss, stroking his tongue with hers, breathing in his breath. Desire was like a fever in her blood, rushing through her veins, gripping her heart.

She felt the wool of his sweater underneath her hands, a frustrating barrier when she already knew the heavenly feel of his skin. Impatiently she pushed up his sweater. One of her hands slipped under it and glided over the smooth, hard planes of his hair-roughened chest. His gasp emboldened her. She couldn't seem to get enough of him. Maybe she never would.

She pulled away from his mouth, but only far enough to tell him what was burning in her heart.

"Changed...my mind," she said. "I want...to make love in the hot tub."

He smiled then, a slow, devastating grin more thrilling than a wild run on the black-diamond trail. He raised her off his lap and set her down on an adjacent sofa cushion before standing and lifting her into his strong arms.

"Honey, I'm all for giving you what you want," he said as he strode to the stairway with long, powerful steps. "If you asked me, I'd even buy you a potbellied pig."

She giggled and buried her face against his chest while he ran up the steps as though she weighed nothing. Why, she wondered, had she initially believed that a big man like Cole wasn't her type?

But even as she acknowledged being thrilled by the way he'd literally swept her off her feet, she understood that Cole's size had nothing to do with her desire for him.

She wanted Cole simply because he was Cole.

She had the sensation of floating as they traveled down the hall, through the door into their bedroom and across the carpet to the French doors that opened onto the wraparound deck. When he set her down beside the

French doors, she couldn't bear to break all contact with him. She caressed his broad back while he worked the lock with fingers that fumbled.

"Nervous?" she asked.

"More like anxious as hell," he growled, and she laughed.

He took her by the hand when he had the door open, and the two of them rushed into the cold air.

"It's freezing," Anna said, wrapping her arms around herself.

"You won't be cold for long," Cole said with one arched eyebrow.

Scooting down, he removed the snow-covered tarp over the hot tub, took something out of his pocket and put it on the ledge near the controls. Then he turned on the jets. The water bubbled and steam rose into the crisp, night air.

"Last one in's an ice cube," Cole said and stripped off his thick sweater.

The snow had stopped shortly after their sleigh ride and the night had cleared. A nearly full moon hung overhead and shone down on the snow. The light bounced off the white blanket, illuminating the deck in a soft glow.

Anna reached for the hem of her sweater but her cold hands stilled. Cole's chest was already bare.

She bit her bottom lip and feasted her eyes on him. He had the muscle definition of a body builder, although his weren't the pumped-up, overblown kind that seasoned competitors exhibited with such aplomb.

They were smoother and sleeker and more beautiful

because of it. A sparse amount of dark hair was sprinkled over the hard planes and knolls of his chest. His skin was shades darker than hers, as though he hadn't completely lost his summer tan.

He made quick work of taking off his shoes, socks and jeans until only his jockey shorts remained. They were plain and white but still the sexiest thing she'd ever seen.

He removed those, too, and still she stared. She'd seen naked men before but none who compared with him. He had washboard abs, long, ropy legs and the most impressive erection she'd ever seen. Especially considering the temperature.

He slipped into the water, settled his long length onto one of the built-in seats and sighed in contentment.

And she still hadn't taken off a stitch of clothing.

He frowned. "You're the ice cube," he said.

Quite suddenly, she felt like one. Her temporary trance broken, she quickly peeled off her clothes.

He watched her, his eyes so hot her icy fingers trembled. She was down to her bra and panties when a stiff wind blew across the deck.

"Brrrrr," she said and launched herself over the side of the hot tub, underwear and all.

Blessed warmth enveloped her as Cole caught her in his arms, laughing all the while.

"I couldn't wait," she said before she threaded her fingers in his hair and pulled his mouth down to hers.

His lips were cool, an exciting contrast to the hot water streaming from the underwater jets. His big hands glided over her slick skin, curving over her buttocks and pulling her onto his lap.

She opened her eyes as she kissed him and found that he was looking back at her. The intimacy was startling.

His eyes were so dark and glazed with passion that she couldn't distinguish his pupils. Last night, when they'd made love with the lights off, she'd reveled in the sense of touch. But now that she could see the effect she had on him, the pleasure doubled. He cupped her breast and a shiver ran the length of her body.

"I love to watch what I do to you," he said, echoing her thoughts.

"You could do more if we got my wet clothes off," she said.

He smiled and reached around her to unhook the clasp of her white lace bra. It floated away on a jet of water, unwanted, unneeded.

His hand traveled over her hip, his thumb hooking at the waistband of her underwear and tugging downward. The wet material bunched but didn't budge.

"Damn," he said.

She laughed. "Let me do it," she said and slid off the panties, which floated away along with the bra.

When she was naked, he lifted her partially out of the water. The frigid air rushed up to meet her but the heat of his mouth was at her breast before she could get chilled.

She heard a roaring but couldn't be sure if it was the turbulence of the water or the mad rush of blood in her ears. She threw her head back as he feasted and saw snowflakes dropping from the sky in a lacy patchwork.

She slid back down his body, immersing herself once again in the sleek softness of the water as the wind whipped around them and the stars sparkled overhead.

"This has nothing to do with work and nothing to do with anyone else," he said, gazing deep into her eyes. "This is just me and you."

"Yes," she said, panting now. She couldn't see anyone but him, couldn't think about anything else. He crowded her mind, filled her senses.

She reached under the water to stroke his hard length, breathing his gasp into her mouth.

"Now," she said.

She was momentarily disoriented when he lifted her from his lap and rose out of the water, like Zeus emerging from the sea.

"What?" she began, but then he bent to retrieve a packet from the ledge of the hot tub. She remembered him taking something out of his pocket and realized it had been a condom.

He'd remembered, once again, when she might have forgotten to protect herself until it was too late. Her heart swelled with gratitude. He ripped open the package, swiftly covered himself and rejoined her in the frothing tub. He sat on one of the built-in seats and pulled her on top of him so that her knees straddled his thighs.

The water churned from the spray of the jets, creating delightfully soothing ripples, but his hands on her wet skin felt better. Unable to wait any longer, she reached under the water, finding him with unerring accuracy. She opened her legs and guided him inside her.

He was such a big man that she marveled she could accommodate him, but he felt perfect, exactly right.

Hot, soothing streams of bubbles churned around them, but the heat was nothing to what they generated together. They moved together, like longtime lovers. He seemed to know exactly when to speed up, change angles.

She clutched at his back as the tension built inside her, her eyes open and trained on his. His eyes were open, too, and she felt as though she could see inside him to the man underneath the handsome exterior.

What she saw was a beautiful man.

That knowledge pushed her over the edge. Her orgasm detonated inside her, sensation on top of overwhelming sensation. He cried out a moment later, and her deep-muscle spasms intensified. They spiraled, seeming to last for endless moments until she finally was spent in his embrace.

There was no use pretending any longer that it wasn't exactly where she wanted to be.

10

COLE SPRAWLED utterly content beneath the downy warmth of the quilt on the king-sized bed. Anna was curled up next to him, her head nestled against his shoulder.

After making love in the hot tub, he'd carried her into the bedroom. They'd been chilled by the time they reached the room, even after drying each other with large, fluffy towels.

Anna had proposed the ideal solution: shared body heat.

So they'd made love again, this time in the big, soft sleigh bed with the lights blazing. Cole was physically and mentally tired, but he wanted her still. He suspected that he always would.

"You were right," she said softly when they were both breathing relatively normally again.

He dropped a kiss on top of her head. "About my belief that you should spend every minute you're with me naked?"

"I kind of like that idea, but that's not it," she said, tilting her head so she could grin up at him. Her expression grew serious almost immediately. "I meant you were right about my family. I was using them to push you away. But I'm still not..."

Her voice trailed off, but he could guess at what she'd been about to say. "You're still not sure you want us to be in a relationship when the vacation's over?"

Her sigh told him he'd hit the mark. Something painful clutched in his chest. He'd been afraid of this last night before they'd ended up in the hot tub together. Could it be that he hadn't gotten across the point that she was more important than any job?

"Don't tell me you still think we can't be co-workers and lovers," he said, striving to keep his apprehension out of his voice.

She drew a long breath. "I have my doubts."

"What doubts?"

She sat up. The covers fell away so that she was exposed from the waist up. Her naked breasts looked lovely in the soft light, but he didn't reach for them. This was more important than sex.

"Let me ask you something." She pulled her silk nightgown over her head and chewed on her bottom lip. "Would you tell me if I asked what was inside your briefcase?"

"My briefcase?" He sat up, dragging a hand through his disheveled hair. "I don't understand."

"I found you alone in the office on Christmas Eve, almost like you didn't want anyone to know what you were doing. You allude to this work you have but I don't know anything about it. You even brought it along on this trip."

"What do you think is in my briefcase?" he asked. When she averted her eyes, the reason struck him like a blow. "You think it's something I don't want you to see.

You think I'm scheming to get your job, that I'm going to bypass you and go straight to the top with my ideas."

"The thought had occurred to me," she admitted.

A spurt of something hot and fitful surged through Cole and he got out of bed, not caring that he was naked. He picked up the briefcase, punched in the combination that unlocked it and dumped the contents on the bed.

Sheets of paper with computer-generated images floated down to the mattress along with pages of copy. He held his breath as he waited for her to say she didn't need to inspect them but instead she picked up one of the papers and examined it. His chest constricted. What had he expected from a woman who didn't trust him?

She gathered up some more of the papers and leafed through them. "These are amended designs for the brochure advertising the tie-in with local ski resorts," she said, almost to herself. Finally she raised her eyes. "I don't understand. I thought you finished that before Christmas."

"Yeah, well, I wasn't completely happy with it," he said. "The brochure hasn't gone into production yet so I thought I'd improve my ideas over the holiday break and present them to you Monday morning."

"This is what you meant on Christmas Eve when you said you had ideas for a new brochure," she said almost to herself.

Guilt descended over her face like rain. Good, he thought. It served her right for believing he was conniving behind her back, except...except that's exactly what he was doing.

He felt sick to his stomach when he realized the extent of his treachery.

It was true that he'd spent a few minutes on Christmas Eve working on the brochure, but the bulk of the time he'd been analyzing the marketing report. On his laptop back at his apartment, he had the company's financial records dating back five years waiting for him to scrutinize.

Anna was mistaken in her belief that he wanted to become Skillington Ski's marketing director. But at his father's bidding, he was trying to figure out if Anna's job performance was costing the company business.

Since he'd come to know Anna and the other fine people who worked for Skillington, he'd resolved to find a way for the company to stay solvent without cutting either jobs or stores. But there was no guarantee he'd succeed. A single word from him could still cost Anna the job she loved so much.

"I'm sorry," she said, real regret in her voice. "I shouldn't have—"

"No, don't." He sat down next to her on the bed and silenced her with three fingers over her lips. He couldn't stand to listen to her ask for forgiveness when he was the one who had sinned. "You don't have to apologize."

Her fingers closed over his wrist and she pulled his hand from her mouth.

"Yes, I do. I shouldn't have doubted you," she said, her eyes clear and earnest as she gazed at him. Another knife of guilt stabbed him. "I should have trusted my instincts about what kind of man you are."

The kind of man who lies to the woman he loves, he agonized. His throat closed and his heart seemed to thud to a stop as the truth rose up inside him.

He loved her.

She ran her fingers softly, almost reverently over his cheek. "I'm willing to give the whole co-worker/lover thing a try." She lowered her eyes, brought them back up again. "If you'll still have me."

He should tell her he was the one who wasn't worthy, but the words stuck in his throat. By confiding in Anna, he'd be betraying his father. That he couldn't do. He'd been brought up to believe that a man was only as good as his word, and he'd given his word to Arthur Skillington that he wouldn't reveal their connection. He couldn't break it, not without compromising everything he'd ever believed in.

"Cole?" she asked in a small voice. Her mouth trembled and the confidence seemed to seep from her. It took him a moment to realize she was waiting for his reply.

He grabbed her by the shoulders, wishing he'd never have to let her go but knowing one day soon he might not have a choice. Would she understand that omitting all the facts from a story wasn't the same as lying? He could only pray that she would.

"Of course I want you," he said. "I always want you."

That, at least, was the truth.

Joy replaced the uncertainty in her eyes and she threw her arms around his neck and kissed his mouth.

Because he couldn't stop himself, he kissed her back. But not before he made himself a promise.

As soon as he contacted his father and discharged his obligation of secrecy, he'd tell Anna he was Arthur Skillington's son.

He'd tell her, because he loved her.

ANNA'S STOMACH JUMPED giddily with every step as she ran lightly up the thickly carpeted stairs in the chalet.

She'd be less than honest with herself if she attributed the giddiness to the impromptu exercise. Her speeding heart told her it had everything to do with Cole.

She not only had a lover who could make her toes curl with a lift of his eyebrow, but a boyfriend.

The last part would take some getting used to. She typically spent much more time getting to know a man before thinking of him in those terms.

She'd never thought of the lying Larry Lipinski that way, and they'd dated for six months. Six months in which she'd kept him far away from her family. She'd always known that bringing a man home to meet her family would have far-reaching consequences. They were so eager for her to have somebody special in her life that they'd embrace whoever she chose.

Cole had not only met her family but won over every last one of them over. For once, she couldn't bring herself to mind.

Even if she didn't know whether he liked his eggs sunny-side up or scrambled.

She wrenched open the bedroom door and stepped inside the room. Cole sat on the edge of the bed in a ray of sunlight shining through the window. His back was to her, his hair still damp from the shower.

"Cole, I know I said I'd make breakfast but I didn't ask—"

He put up his right index finger to silence her. Only then did she notice that he had a cell phone to his ear.

"Are you sure there's not a mistake?" he asked and nodded slowly at whatever the person on the other end of the line told him. "Could you check again?"

He drummed the fingers of his left hand on the bed, which struck Anna as atypical. She'd worked with Cole for more than a month and couldn't remember seeing him exhibit any signs of agitation.

"I see," he said after a minute. He absently scratched his head. "Yes, maybe I will call back. Thanks for your help."

After he clicked off the phone, his shoulders rose and fell. But his face was impassive, as though he was deliberately masking his worry.

"Is everything okay?" she asked, walking the rest of the way toward him.

"Everything's fine."

"From that phone call, it didn't sound like everything was fine."

"Oh, that." He paused and a dozen possibilities of who he might have called popped into her head. He seemed to choose his next words with care. "I'm having a hard time reaching my dad but I'm sure it's nothing to worry about."

The uneasiness that had been pressing at her chest

lifted. She'd been afraid he had been trying to contact another woman, Anna realized. But he hadn't.

"Which dad? The one in the Bahamas with your mom or the one in Hawaii?"

"The dad in Hawaii," he answered.

"But it's something like four o'clock in the morning in Hawaii."

"Four twenty-one, according to the desk clerk," he said. "I didn't think about the time difference before I called."

"Did the desk clerk refuse to ring his room because it was too early?"

He shook his head, and she got the distinct impression this was a topic he didn't want to discuss. But why? "He said he wasn't registered. I must have remembered the name of his hotel wrong."

"Can you try him on his cell phone?"

Cole shook his head. "He won't carry one. Says he doesn't want to be available to anybody twenty-four hours a day."

"That's what Mr. Skillington says, too," Anna said. Cole's head snapped up and she could read the worry on his face. "Is it really that important you reach him to-day?"

"Important?" He shook his head vigorously. "Nah. It's not important. I wanted to say hello, see how things are going, is all. Not important. Not important at all."

He's holding something back, Anna thought. There's something he doesn't want me to know. No sooner did she have the thoughts than guilt poked through her suspicion. She'd imagined the worse over the contents of his briefcase and look how that had turned out. He'd never been anything but honest with her. Maybe it was time to give him the benefit of the doubt.

"I'm sure your father's fine," Anna said. "It's probably hard to be in Hawaii and not have a good time."

"You're probably right." Cole tousled his hair, which was starting to curl at the ends as it dried, but he still seemed preoccupied. "Was there something you wanted to ask me?"

"Just if you like your eggs scrambled or sunny-side up," she said.

She watched as he refocused his attention on her and smiled, as though he'd consciously decided not to worry about his father for the time being.

"You've got a lot to learn about me if you're asking a question like that." Cole rose and slung his arm around her shoulders. The gesture was friendly, but her reaction to him was purely sexual. She had to fight not to shiver. "You don't get as big as I am by being picky about your food."

She laughed. "I take it that means you don't have a preference."

"Sure, I do. I like my eggs hot." His eyes danced. "Like my women."

He steered her out the door and down the hall before she could tell him she'd be just as happy to stay in the room. It was just as well. Woman could not live on sex alone.

"How are you going to eat your eggs?" he asked.

"I'm not having any. I usually have yogurt or a piece of fruit for breakfast."

"If you don't eat more than that this morning, you won't have enough energy to make it down the ski slope."

She tipped her head so she could see his face. "You want to go skiing today?"

"And keep you from enjoying your last day on the slopes?" He gave a self-deprecating laugh. "No way. We can catch up later."

A day of uninterrupted skiing, something she didn't get to do nearly enough, sounded heavenly. "But what will you do?"

"I thought I'd work."

Even though he'd showed her what he was working on last night, his answer sent a shiver of unease through her. How much tweaking could he do to a job she'd thought was nearly perfect to begin with?

"So you're planning to work all day?" she asked slowly.

He gave her a rueful grin. "Not all day. The Cub Scouts begged me to meet them on the tubing hill at two o'clock."

"And you're actually considering it?" she asked incredulously. "Don't you realize it's ten degrees colder today with a good chance of more snow?"

"The biggest man on the mountain's got to do what the biggest man on the mountain's got to do," he said with a shrug so easygoing she felt thoroughly ashamed of herself.

Cole might be ambitious, but he was also a good, honorable man. Sneak attacks weren't his style. If he meant to move in on her job any time soon, he'd tell her.

Their relationship wouldn't stand a chance if she didn't trust him to be up-front with her. Wasn't his honesty one of the things that had drawn her to him in the first place?

Instead of doubting him, she should look for opportunities to support him. Surely Skillington Ski was big enough for the both of them.

"Cole Mansfield," she said, hugging onto his arm. "You are an incredible man."

"Incredibly lucky," he said before he stopped, turned her into his arms and kissed her so thoroughly that there was no more room for doubt.

"OKAY, I GIVE UP." Cole smiled indulgently as he leaned back against the headboard of the bed and linked his fingers behind his neck. "Why are you so excited about dinner at the lodge?"

Anna balanced on one foot as she pulled a shoe onto the other. She wore a dressy black pantsuit with a long jacket and tapered pants that made her legs seem gazelle-long but still he longed for summer.

Irwin Shaw had it right. There was something magical about girls in their summer dresses. He very much wanted to see Anna in a gauzy slip of fabric that bared her long, beautiful limbs. Not that he'd wish for her to keep the dress on for long.

"I'm excited because we're having dinner together," Anna said. "You haven't eaten at the lodge's better restaurant yet. You'll love it. I highly recommend the teriyaki top sirloin."

She smiled at him in a way that made it seem as

though she was directly in the path of a sunbeam. She'd done a lot of smiling since returning from her day on the slopes. He wanted to believe he made her happy but sensed there was more to it.

"Why else are you excited about tonight?" he prompted.

"How do you know there is another reason?"

"Besides the way your eyes darted away when I just asked you?"

She rolled her eyes and shook her head, the affability never leaving her expression.

"Geez," she said. "Can't you leave a girl in peace to plan a surprise?"

He rubbed his palms together, grinning. "A surprise? I like the sound of that. Does it involve nudity?"

She picked up a throw pillow off the embroidered wing chair in the corner of the room and tossed it at him. He caught it easily.

"It won't be much of a surprise if I tell you what it is, now will it?"

"Okay, okay." He crossed his legs at the ankles. "As long as you're not planning a bait and switch, I can live with that."

"What do you mean a bait and switch?"

"Would you believe the Cub Scouts are cooking around the campfire tonight?" he said and gave a mock shiver. "This is their winter camping trip. They invited me but I draw the line at cooking outside when the temperature dips below sixty degrees."

"Sixty? It's not even thirty out there."

"Exactly," Cole said.

"Wimp," she said, but her voice was affectionate.

She came over to sit on the edge of the bed. "Speaking of cold and snow, you didn't tell me about your day. Did you have fun tubing with your little buddies?"

"It was okay." He tried to hide a groan.

"I heard that," she said. "What happened?"

He held up his hands. "I want to get it straight first off that it wasn't my fault. I didn't know what was going on back there."

"What happened?" she asked again, a sparkle of anticipation in her dark eyes.

He didn't want to tell her, not when the story didn't cast him in the best light. But the next thing he knew, the embarrassing tale poured out of him.

"I started down the hill, thinking I was pulling the usual five or six kids," he said. "Turned out there were ten of them back there. We sped down that hill so fast, we almost flattened this mom who went down before us. She got out of her tube just before we sent it flying."

"Oh, no."

"Oh, yes. I was yelling at people to clear out. We might never have stopped if we hadn't crashed into the netting at the bottom of the hill."

A shudder passed through him at the memory. He'd taken the brunt of the jarring stop. The kids trailing him had bounced off the tubes in front and behind them. Their gleeful yells had been so loud, they'd probably shattered eardrums all over the mountain.

"That doesn't sound good."

"It got worse after the supervisor hunted me down," he said glumly. "He was this little guy with an accent I couldn't quite place. He stood toe-to-toe with me and shouted, 'No more tubing for you.'"

Anna's eyes danced, her lips twitched and laughter bubbled from her. He watched in exasperation as it came out of her in great waves.

"It was damn embarrassing," he said indignantly.

"I'm sure...it...was...." She was laughing so hard she was hardly intelligible.

Cole glared at her. "What?"

"It's just...so funny." She laughed harder, then made an effort to control herself. She scooted over and laid a hand on his arm. "I have this mental picture of this tiny supervisor bawling you out while you stand there all cool in your all-black ski clothes. Only you're not a rebel without a cause. You're a rebel without a tube."

A gurgle of laughter tried to escape him, but he swallowed it back. He gripped her arms and flipped her over so that she lay on her back.

"You think that's funny?" he asked, supporting himself on his elbows.

Her eyes swam with tears of laughter as she burst into fresh mirth. "Very funny," she said.

Cole's day had been frustrating for reasons other than the tubing incident. He'd neither been able to concentrate on work nor locate Arthur Skillington in Hawaii.

But now, looking down at Anna's lovely, laughing face, his worries melted away and his lips twitched.

"Admit it," she urged. "It's funny."

His laugh started in his belly and rumbled upward.

He let the laughter get the best of him and weakly rested his forehead against hers.

When their chortles finally died down, he lifted his head. A smile still touched her lips and her eyes shone, like the moonlight on a clear, wintry night.

Supporting himself on one elbow, he traced the sweep of her cheek and the curve of her jaw.

"Ah, Anna, I think I'm falling in love with you."

He hadn't meant to say that, not before he'd contacted his father and straightened out the whole Skillington Ski mess. But his heart had been so full of her, he simply couldn't hold back the words.

Her smile vanished, her brow wrinkled and she caught her bottom lip between small, white teeth. His heart seized while interminable seconds passed. He held his breath while he waited for her to respond. Finally, she sighed.

"Damn it all."

Everything inside him seemed to deflate. His disappointment was so staggering that it was hard for him to draw a breath.

"Here's a piece of advice," he said when he trusted his voice not to shake. "The next time a man tells you something like that, find a more humane way to break his heart."

She blinked. "You think I'm breaking your heart?"

He tried a smile, didn't manage it. "You already broke it."

"But I think I'm falling in love with you, too!"

Something bright and hopeful leaped in his chest, but

he couldn't let it loose. Not yet. "Then why were you damning it all?"

"Because my family's big on saying 'I told you so.'"

His grin started small and grew in similar proportion to the one creasing her face. For long moments, they gazed at each other, acknowledging the bond between them.

Then he lowered his head and she lifted her lips.

She tasted of the minty toothpaste she'd used while getting ready for dinner and smelled like strawberry-scented shampoo. She felt like a daydream, her body rich and lush beneath his questing hands, her soft breasts pressing against his chest.

Except in his fantasy, she wasn't wearing nearly as many clothes. He drew back, his fingers going to the buttons on her jacket.

"What are you doing?" she said, her breaths uneven.

"Taking off your clothes," he said as he got her jacket open and started on the buttons of her shirt.

"But we have—" she gasped as his fingers brushed the flesh exposed above her bra "—dinner reservations."

"They can wait." He unclasped her bra, letting her breasts spill free. Half-dressed, with her creamy white skin a contrast to the black of her pantsuit, she was a vision.

He put his mouth to the rosy tip of one breast, teasing the peak into a hard nub, relishing the slightly salty taste of her soft skin. She fastened her hands in his hair, holding him in place while she emitted sexy little moans.

He finally worked his way back up to her mouth, kissing the valley between her breasts and every inch of flesh along the way. She met him with openmouthed abandon, her tongue dipping to taste him.

He stroked the length of her upper body, insinuating a hand between them so he could unbutton her pants. His fingers worked the zipper, and then his hand roamed over her flat belly and ventured inside her panties, finding her already wet and ready for him. He dipped two fingers inside her and she moaned against his mouth.

"C-Cole," she said brokenly.

He lifted his head so he could look at her, enjoying the high color on her cheeks, the glaze in her eyes.

"We'll be late for dinner," she finished.

He tipped his head bemusedly, because his appetite wasn't for dinner. The way she was staring at him, with eyes that had gone almost black, hers didn't seem to be, either.

But it appeared important to her that they get to the restaurant more or less on time.

He grinned at her rakishly.

"Then let's make this quick," he said.

He sat up, threw off his own dinner jacket and quirked an eyebrow. "We can start by racing to see who can get naked first."

She won, possibly because he already had her half undressed but he wouldn't discount the shakiness of his hands.

They were steady and sure, however, when he put on a condom and pulled her on top of him.

The feel of her naked skin against his was so enthralling that he wanted to bury himself in her almost immediately, but he didn't. A clarification of what he'd said earlier clamored in his brain, begging to get out.

He threaded his hands through her hair, holding her head in place as he spoke what was in his heart.

"Before, when I said I thought I was falling in love with you, that wasn't quite true." He took a breath, wanting to dispel the clouds that had appeared in her eyes. "I am in love with you."

Her face lit up, like the sunny summer days he favored. She smiled, her heart in her eyes, and he took a mental snapshot of the way she looked so he'd never forget this moment.

"I love you, too," she said before their bodies did the rest of the talking for them.

Without the need for a single additional word, they expressed the intensity of their love for each other quite eloquently.

11

ANNA TUGGED on his hand as they navigated the wood-paneled hall leading to Snow Caps, the pricey restaurant on the upper floor of the ski lodge that overlooked slopes that reflected the glow of the moon.

Cole's stride was long but she set the pace, which was just shy of warp speed.

"We have to hurry, Cole," she called over her shoulder. "We're already late."

The first time she'd dressed for the evening, before they'd made love, she'd looked coolly sophisticated. Now her color was high, her hair delicately mussed and her lips chapped, but not from the cold temperature outside.

He vastly preferred this look.

"Hurry," she said again, tugging harder.

He picked up the pace, only now remembering what she'd said earlier about a surprise. He'd gotten the impression the surprise had to do with dinner.

Had she ordered a special dish? Arranged for the waiters to serenade them? Paid for somebody to pop out of their dessert?

Whatever the surprise, it couldn't compare with the gift of love they'd given each other before dinner. The night was so magical because of it that, for once, he wasn't going to let his secret worry him.

He'd tell her the truth soon enough. Until then, he needed to believe she loved him enough to understand.

Anna was nearly out of breath when they reached the black-jacketed maître d'. He looked up expectantly from the seating plan he'd been studying.

"I have a table reserved for Wesley," Anna said, her words coming in sexy bursts. "For four."

The maître d' sniffed disapprovingly, probably because they were late, but kept from remarking on their tardiness.

"Follow me," he said in clipped tones.

Before complying, Anna turned to Cole with an excited smile.

"Let me guess," he said. "Our dinner companions are the surprise."

When she nodded, everything clicked into place. That's why she'd been so concerned about getting to the restaurant on time. She hadn't wanted to keep whoever it was waiting.

"You can thank me after dinner," she said.

He lifted his eyebrows and ran his hand down her arm. "I can think of the perfect way."

She giggled. "I'll hold you to that."

Smiling, he placed his hand at the small of her back and guided her through the maze of tables. Flickers of candlelight at the center of each table lent the restaurant a romantic air which was reinforced by the formal dress of the wait staff.

The restaurant was perfect for lovers. Cole regretted

that he and Anna wouldn't be alone until she turned and gave him another excited smile. Whoever was waiting for them must surely be someone he wanted to see.

The maître d' stopped at a table a few paces away and set down menus at the empty place settings with a flourish. When he stepped out of Cole's line of vision, the tall, gray-haired man sitting alone at the table came into view.

Cole's breath caught while the blood drained from his face.

It was Arthur Skillington.

"Cole?" His father's openmouthed, monosyllabic greeting alerted Cole that he wasn't the only one who'd gotten a shock.

"You two know each other?" Anna asked, then gave a little laugh. "But of course you do. Mr. Skillington hasn't been in the office much recently, but you met him when you were hired. Right, Cole?"

Anna didn't seem to expect Cole to reply. She pulled out a chair, sat down and addressed his father.

"I'm so sorry we're late, sir. We just—" she gave Cole a guilty glance "—lost track of time. I hope you haven't been waiting long."

Arthur cleared his throat. For one of the first times since Cole had known him, he seemed to be at a loss for words.

Like father, like son, Cole thought.

"Cole, I ran into Mr. Skillington today at the ski lift and invited him to have dinner with us. He and his wife had to change their vacation plans because the airports were snowed in." She turned to his father. "Where were you going again?"

"Hawaii," Arthur answered.

Her hand flew to her chest. "What a coincidence. That's where Cole's father is."

When she directed her attention to him, Cole had the sick feeling that she'd figured it out. But she only frowned and asked, "Aren't you going to sit down, Cole?"

"Yes, by all means, sit," Arthur said, and Cole found the will to move if not to speak.

"It's been such a busy day," Anna babbled on, possibly because nobody else was talking. "Cole spent part of it working on those ideas I was telling you about. He's so talented at what he does. His work is simply marvelous...."

Cole couldn't focus on the rest of her words because he'd already grasped the gist of them. Anna was trying to make him look good, ostensibly to help his career, possibly at the expense of her own.

Because she loved him.

He met his father's questioning glance across the table and tried to get his vocal cords to work. He needed to say something before Arthur did.

"But where are my manners," Anna said, still talking way too fast. "I haven't even asked why your wife isn't joining us. Is she okay?"

"I'm fine, Anna. I was in the rest room, is all."

All three of them turned toward the new arrival. Lilly Skillington, elegant in gray silk pants and a white embroidered sweater shot through with silver threads, approached the table.

Lilly smiled graciously at Anna, then turned expectantly to Cole. Surprise and pleasure registered in her expression.

"Why, Cole, I didn't know you'd be here."

Cole felt as helpless as an animal caught in the headlights of an approaching car to prevent what he knew would happen next.

Anna's gaze swung from him back to Lilly. "You two know each other?"

"Of course we know each other," Lilly replied. "Cole is Arthur's son."

ANNA'S BRAIN DIDN'T WANT to process what her ears had heard.

Arthur Skillington's wife had to be mistaken. Cole couldn't be the boss's son. For one thing, his last name was Mansfield. For another, heirs to the throne didn't masquerade as the king's subjects.

"No," she said, shaking her head as if that would make it untrue. "Cole isn't a Skillington."

Lilly laughed lightly as she pulled out her chair and sat down. "He might not use the last name, but I assure you he's a Skillington. Look at them. Can't you see the family resemblance?"

Arthur Skillington was tall and broad, exactly the kind of man who might once have been a football lineman. His dark hair had begun to gray and his chiseled features and blue eyes reminded her of somebody. That somebody, she realized with a start, was Cole.

Cole, who'd come to western Pennsylvania to establish a connection with his biological father.

How could she have been such a fool?

"Anna, I can explain," Cole said urgently.

"No, son. I'll explain," Arthur Skillington interjected. "Anna, it's important that you don't let on at work that Cole is my son."

Her mouth opened but no sound came out.

"It'll come as a surprise to you that Skillington Ski has been having financial difficulty. I asked Cole to figure out why."

She cleared her throat and forced her question past the lump clogging her windpipe. "You mean you asked him to spy on us?"

"No, no." Mr. Skillington waved his hand in a characteristic gesture reminiscent of his son. "I wanted Cole to get the lay of the land. An insider's view that would be impossible if anyone knew he was my son. I need his input before I can make…changes."

His hesitation clued Anna that some of those changes would involve personnel. She felt as though she'd been struck, especially because guilt was written all over Cole, as clearly as if the word had been stenciled on his forehead in black marker.

"You never wanted my job for yourself, did you?" She addressed the question to Cole. "You wanted to see if I was worthy of keeping it."

"It wasn't like that, Anna," he said in a low, insistent voice, but Anna had heard enough.

"Mr. Skillington, Mrs. Skillington," she said, looking

at them, looking anywhere but at Cole. "If you'll excuse me, suddenly I'm not feeling very well."

She got up and walked out of the restaurant, her head held regally high. She was not the one who had anything to be ashamed of, but that didn't seem to matter to her heart. It was still splintering.

She supposed she expected Cole to make his excuses to the Skillingtons—correction, his father and step-mother—and chase after her. But she still wasn't prepared to deal with him when he caught up to her outside the restaurant.

"Anna, stop."

He put a hand on her arm, but she shook it off and kept on walking.

One side of the deserted hallway featured large, double-paned windows that afforded a view of the snow-covered landscape. The moon was full tonight, its light reflecting off the snow to create a postcard-perfect view.

Anna barely saw it through her welling tears. She blinked them back and focused on her anger. She needed to keep it alive to get through this with her dignity.

"Anna." Cole's voice was pleading this time. "We need to talk about this."

"Why?" The angry word erupted from her. "So you can laugh at me for trying to help your career? Or lie to me about how you weren't putting my job in jeopardy?"

"This isn't about the job," he growled.

She stopped walking and whirled on him. "How can

you say that? Weren't you listening when I told you how much that job means to me?"

"This isn't about the job," he repeated. "It's about us."

"There is no us." She shook her head against the pain her denial caused. The anguish was reflected in his face, but she steeled herself against it.

"How can you say that after tonight?" he asked. "You told me you loved me."

"I told Cole Mansfield I loved him, not Cole Skillington."

"My name is Cole Mansfield." He ran a hand through his hair. "I never lied to you about that. I met Arthur seven months ago, exactly like I told you."

"That doesn't excuse what you did."

He bent his head so it was closer to hers. She stepped back and felt the chill of the night through the windowpane, the same chill invading her heart.

"Didn't you listen to what Arthur said, Anna? His business is barely breaking even. He instructed me not to let anyone know we were related. I gave him my word. What was I supposed to do?"

"You weren't supposed to sleep with one of the people you were spying on. Or maybe you were. Maybe it was part of your master plan to sleep with the boss."

"That's crazy, Anna. You're the one who invited me over on Christmas Eve. I didn't plan any of this." He lowered his voice. "I didn't plan the way I feel about you."

Because she felt her defenses weakening, she

snapped at him. "Save it, Cole. I won't listen to any more of your lies."

He took a step toward her, effectively pinning her back against the glass of the window, and laid a hand on her cheek.

"It's not a lie," he said. "I love you."

She blinked back tears and batted at his hand so that it fell away from her skin.

"If you loved me, you would have told me the truth."

"I was going to—"

"When?" she interrupted. "After you made your report to your father and the ax fell on my job? Is that when you were finally going to tell me?"

"I couldn't tell you until I let my father know I needed to break my promise," he said. "That's why I was on the phone this morning trying to locate him."

"Do you think it would have made any difference, Cole? I'm not an idiot. I realize where you and your father are heading with this. You're a Skillington. He wants you as his right-hand man. The minute you stepped into his life, my job was history."

He clenched his jaw and raised his eyes toward the ceiling. "Why do you keep bringing up the job? Can't you see the job has nothing to do with this?"

"It has everything to do with it." Anna lifted her chin, willing her lips not to quiver. "The job is what's important to me."

He reeled back as though he'd been struck. "Funny," he said, an odd catch in his voice, "but I got the impression when we were in bed together that I was important to you."

She braced herself against the agony in his voice, telling herself it couldn't be as sincere as it sounded.

"I already told you, Cole. Back there, I didn't even know who you were," she said. "You're certainly not the man I told I loved."

He retreated another step, leaving her free to move away from the window. Her back felt cold from where it had touched the glass, a chill that permeated her entire body.

She and Cole were silent, their eyes locked on each other, as a trio of men walked by, talking loudly about their exploits that afternoon on the slopes.

She watched Cole's jaw harden, his expression turn icy and thought she might never be warm again.

"If that's how you feel," he said when the men were out of earshot, "we don't have anything more to say to each other."

"I agree," she said even as she wanted to call back her words.

She couldn't love him. She wouldn't let herself.

"Give me fifteen minutes and I'll have my things out of the chalet," he said.

He remained immobile after making the declaration, as though giving her the opportunity to protest.

Don't go, her heart cried.

She stubbornly refused to listen to it.

"Fine," she said.

He searched her eyes but she firmed her jaw and refused to look away. Finally, with a rueful shake of his head, he pivoted and strode down the hall. She watched him go, his figure growing smaller and smaller until he disappeared down the stairs.

As she gazed out the window into the cold, barren landscape, a single tear trickled down her cheek. She wiped away the frigid drop of moisture with the pads of her fingers until it was gone, like her hopes for the future and the man she had so foolishly loved.

12

SILVER-AND-GOLD STREAMERS hung from the chandelier while helium balloons in an array of colors bobbed gently against the ceiling.

Across one wall, a gaily colored banner proclaimed: I'll Make It To The New Year Or Die Trying. The house was alive with conversation and the soft strains of music while people milled about tossing back drinks and munching on hors d'oeuvres.

All was as it should be at the Wesleys' annual New Year's Eve Party. The only thing out of whack was Anna's mood, which was decidedly not festive.

It had been two days since she'd discovered Cole for the schemer he was and nearly forty-eight hours since he'd cleared out of the chalet.

She deliberately affixed a bright smile to her face as she carried a tray of hors d'oeuvres into the living area.

Nobody would know she was pining after Cole if she could help it, not when she was so angry with herself for failing to put him out of her mind.

She'd barely made it into the living room when Grandma Ziemanski headed toward her, like a homing pigeon on speed.

Her silver dress, which she wore every New Year's

Eve, was covered with so many spangles and sparkles that Anna was temporarily blinded.

"I'll take one of those." Grandma Ziemanski plucked a piece of sauce-drenched kielbasa off the tray by the toothpick sticking from it. She popped it into her mouth. "Not half bad. Did you make these?"

Anna nodded. "Weren't you the one who saw to it that all the Ziemanski women could cook?"

"You know what they say about the way to a man's heart." Grandma smirked. "Not that there's any truth to that once you get a man in the bedroom."

Anna put a hand to her chest and pretended to be shocked. "Grandma, please."

When her grandmother chuckled, she knew the older woman had been angling for exactly that reaction.

"Speaking of men who'd look darn good in the bedroom, when is your Cole getting here?"

Anna stiffened but managed to keep her smile in place. "He's not coming."

"What do you mean he's not coming?"

Her grandmother sounded indignant.

"Do you know how long we've been waiting for you to have a man in your life? What kind of boyfriend is he if he won't spend New Year's Eve with you?"

Anna set the tray down on the nearest table, scolding herself for delaying this moment. She should have set her family straight about Cole once and for all but she'd avoided contact with them since returning from the ski vacation.

She'd begged off their invitations, instead staying tat home and burying herself in work. As though brainstorming a list of new marketing strategies to pull Skill-ington Ski out of the doldrums would do her any good.

She fully expected to lose her job, possibly as early as the day after New Year's. The prospect still wrenched at her, but at least she wouldn't have to deal with Cole any longer. She wasn't sure she could survive another en-counter with him without crying.

"Cole isn't my boyfriend, Grandma."

"Sure he is." Grandma's lipstick-pink mouth thinned into a tight line. "You brought him home on Christmas Eve. You took him along on the ski vacation. You even gave him a thong."

Anna pinched the bridge of her nose, trying to stave off the headache she felt coming on.

"I made some mistakes," she said. "But Cole isn't my boyfriend. He never was."

"I don't believe you," Grandma said stubbornly, puff-ing up her chest.

"It's true, Grandma." Julie appeared as if out of thin air. She wore black, which was appropriate to Anna's mood. In contrast, her hair seemed more red than it usually did. "Cole never was Anna's boyfriend."

Anna gaped at her sister. "If you knew that, why did you make sure he came along on the ski trip?"

"Because I think he's the right man for you," Julie said. "Too bad you're not smart enough to figure that out for yourself."

"You don't know what you're talking about," Anna said, her voice a low hiss. "You don't know what hap-pened between us."

"Whatever it was, I hope it was worth losing the man

you love over," Julie said with obvious sadness before walking away.

Grandma lifted another hors d'oeuvre off a passing tray. "I don't get it," she said, waving the delicious morsel at Anna. "If you're in love with Cole, then why isn't he your boyfriend?"

"I'm not..." Anna began, but the words wouldn't come. "Oh, never mind," she said and walked away. She filled a glass from the punch bowl she knew was spiked and took a big gulp.

"Hey, Anna," Grandpa Ziemanski called to her from across the table. Light from an overhead chandelier made his bald head gleam. "Let me know when Cole gets here. I've gotta show him this."

He held up a diapered doll with a banner across its bare chest that proclaimed it the New Year's Baby. When he squeezed the doll's tummy, it counted down from ten, then let out a high-pitched squeal.

Grandpa laughed merrily before heading across the room. "Hey," he yelled to her unsuspecting cousins. "You gotta see this."

Her mother bustled by, an empty tray in hand. "Cole's late," she said. "You need to cure him of that."

Her father appeared at her elbow and whispered, "Let the boy have his vices, Anna. Either that, or he'll hide them from you."

Anna took another gulp of punch, not even caring if it was one of those varieties that stained your tongue red. It was time she set her father straight.

"Dad, I—"

A doorbell chimed, closely followed by the sound of

the door opening and closing. Her father winked at her. "Maybe that's your fella now."

Surely Cole wouldn't crash their New Year's Eve party, Anna thought. Except...maybe he would. He'd shown up at the chalet when she hadn't expected him. Maybe crashing was his thing.

Anna's heart thudded while she watched the entry to the living room. Interminable seconds seemed to pass before she saw...Aunt Miranda and Uncle Peter. Their arms were around each other's waists, their mouths curved in matching smiles.

Aunt Miranda, resplendent in a ruby-red dress, laughed at something Uncle Peter said. He bent to kiss her full on the lips.

"I thought they were fighting," Anna said.

"They obviously got over that," her father remarked before heading off to greet the new arrivals.

Just what I need, Anna thought, even as she felt a spurt of joy that her aunt and uncle had managed to mend their marriage. *Lovebirds in my midst.*

She was tempted to skulk away to hide her own pain, but Aunt Miranda spotted her. She tore herself away from Uncle Peter and tottered toward Anna on too-high heels. Anna nearly choked on a cloud of perfume as her aunt enveloped her in a warm hug.

"What was that all about?" Anna asked with a be-mused smile when Aunt Miranda released her.

"I'm not sure." Aunt Miranda looked sheepish. "Sharing the happiness, maybe. Where's Cole?"

"Not here," Anna said. Her aunt tilted her head, obviously expecting more of an explanation. But maybe, finally, Anna was talking to someone who'd understand. "We had a falling-out over work. You know how that goes."

The corners of Aunt Miranda's perfectly outlined lips dipped. "I'm not sure I do. What do you mean?"

"Just that you and Uncle Peter, well, you've had your share of arguments over his job. I'm glad you worked the last one out."

"You thought Peter and I were arguing over his job?" Aunt Miranda let out a short, shocked laugh. "It was never about that."

"Then what was it about?"

Her aunt laid long-nailed fingers on Anna's arm and lowered her voice. "I thought Peter was having an affair. I found a woman's phone number in the pocket of his jacket when I took it to the dry cleaner. He started coming home late, saying he'd been at work. I put two and two together and got three."

"But the answer's four."

"Exactly. Turns out the number belonged to a cleaning woman somebody had recommended. Peter worked late all those nights because I was so nasty to him. He buried himself in his computer while we were at White Tower to avoid dealing with me."

Anna rubbed at the back of her neck, wondering how she'd misinterpreted what was wrong between her aunt and uncle. "How did you find all this out?"

"Simple. I asked him," Aunt Miranda said.

"But how did you know he was telling the truth?"

"Because I knew in my heart I could trust him." She laid a smooth hand on Anna's cheek. "When you love somebody, sometimes you have to take that leap of faith."

"Hey, Anna." Uncle Peter greeted her with a smile, then claimed his wife by the elbow. "I hope you don't mind if I steal my wife for a few minutes. Grandpa Ziemanski has something he wants to show us."

"Not at all," Anna muttered absently. She sank into a chair the moment they headed off, her aunt's words ringing in her mind.

It was never about work. I knew in my heart I could trust him. When you love somebody, you have to take that leap of faith.

She could picture Cole in the hall at the ski lodge, insisting that their situation wasn't about work.

He was right, she belatedly realized. Her conflict with him had never been about work. It hadn't been about her relatives, either.

It was about trusting him enough to let him into a life that included a large, interfering family. The way she didn't trust Brad Perriman, who lied about his marital status. Or Larry Lipinski, who lied about everything else.

Cole wasn't a liar. Neither was he the sort of man who broke his word to somebody he loved. Isn't that why he hadn't told her Arthur Skillington was his father?

She covered her face with her hands.

Cole hadn't lied to her, but she'd lied to herself by making everything about her job.

"What have I done?" she murmured to herself.

"Anna, are you okay?"

She wiped her eyes and found her sister standing over her, concern written so starkly on her face that her freckles stood out like pine cones on snow.

"No, I'm not all right," Anna said, sniffling. "I knew in my heart he was telling the truth, but I wouldn't believe him."

Julie settled her hands on her hips. "So what are you going to do about it?"

Anna blinked to keep at bay the tears forming behind her eyes. "What can I do?"

"Didn't you tell me Arthur Skillington invited you to *his* New Year's Eve party?"

"You think I should go?"

"You love Cole, don't you?"

"Yes," Anna said softly, then with more conviction. "Yes."

Her sister raised her eyebrows but she didn't need to say another word. Anna knew what she had to do.

It was time she took that leap of faith and past time she made it clear that love was more important than any job.

ARTHUR SKILLINGTON CLASPED a large hand on Cole's shoulder and bent his graying head close to his son's. Looking into his dark-blue eyes, Cole thought, was like looking into a mirror. So many things about himself made sense since he'd found his father, not the least of which was why he had a soft heart encased in a hard exterior.

Not far from them, couples danced on the portable floor his father had rented for the occasion. An inebriated guest blew into a horn in premature celebration. Considering Arthur and Lilly had thrown together the party at the last minute, the turnout was impressive.

"Are you sure about this, son?" Arthur asked in a serious voice at odds with the revelry around them.

"As sure as I've ever been about anything," Cole said. "I can't work at Skillington Ski any longer."

Even amid the noise, Cole heard the disappointment in his father's sigh. It made him feel like sighing himself.

"You're positive you don't want to take the weekend to think this over?" Arthur asked. "Talk about it on Monday when your head is clearer?"

Cole shook his head. "I won't change my mind. I need Anna to know that it was never about the job. This is the only way I can think of to prove it."

"Hey, Arthur, come over here and settle an argument for us," yelled a silver-haired man whose cheeks were florid from drink. "Is Dick Clark a descendant of Dorian Gray's?"

Arthur held up one finger, his eyes still fastened on his son's. "You picked a hell of a time to spring this on me."

"I'm sorry," Cole said, meaning it. "But once I made up my mind, I couldn't wait. It was like the knowledge of what I had to do was burning a hole inside me."

Arthur puffed his cheeks with air, then blew it out so they flattened. "You really love this woman, don't you?"

Cole nodded once. "I do."

His father patted his shoulder. "I can't pretend I'm

not disappointed about your resignation. Finding out you're my son was like a miracle. I wanted Skillington Ski to be my legacy to you."

Cole's throat thickened. He cleared it. "Just because I'm not going to work at Skillington anymore doesn't mean you'll lose me."

"I better not," Arthur said gruffly.

Cole clenched his teeth against the emotion welling in his throat. "I've got to go."

"I know," Arthur said an instant before he pulled Cole to him in a spontaneous bear hug. "You've turned into a fine young man, son," he whispered into his ear. "I couldn't be any prouder if I'd raised you myself."

When he was free of Arthur's embrace, Cole gave him a final nod, then threaded his way through the party to the exit.

He blinked to dispel the moisture that had gathered in his eyes, then squared his shoulders and went out into the night.

AN ATTRACTIVE YOUNG MAN wearing a foil party hat and a goofy grin opened the door to Arthur Skillington's sprawling Victorian home and gestured for Anna to come inside.

"You looking to have a good time?" he asked in an affable slur. The strong smell of alcohol on his breath caused her to lean backward.

"Not tonight," she said primly.

"Okay." Without losing the smile, he pointed to a pretty, dark-haired woman about six feet from them. "You think she's looking to have a good time?"

He took off before she could answer, leaving Anna free to follow the noise and the music to a large, expensive-looking room distinguished by a cathedral ceiling and a gleaming wood floor. Arthur Skillington stood out from the crowd of party guests, standing head and shoulders above most of them.

Now that she knew Cole was Mr. Skillington's son, she was surprised she hadn't picked up on the connection before. Both men were tall and muscular with long, straight noses and almost regal bearing. Their coloring, too, was similar: that striking combination of dark hair and blue eyes.

She failed to find Cole during a visual sweep of the room, but he wasn't the man she was seeking. She squared her shoulders, took a breath for courage and headed straight for his father. He was talking to two other men, both of whom seemed prone to great guffaws of laughter.

"Mr. Skillington," she said, but he didn't hear her. She repeated his name, finally resorting to tugging on his sleeve to get his attention. He turned toward her, eyes reminiscent of Cole's widening in surprise.

"Anna," he exclaimed. "Lilly said you weren't coming."

"I didn't expect to come, sir, but I need to talk to you," Anna said. "It can't wait."

"There's a lot of impatience going around tonight," he said mysteriously, then made his excuses to the laughing men he'd been talking to. He walked her to a relatively quiet corner of the party.

"Why don't you take off your coat, stay a while?"

She looked down at herself, only then realizing she still wore her red winter coat. "I can't," she said. "What I have to say won't take long."

"Okay, then. What's so important that you need to tell it to me at..." he checked his gold watch "...eleven-fifty on New Year's Eve?"

"I need to resign my position at Skillington." The job had been important to Anna for so long that she was surprised at how easy it was to state her intention. "Effective immediately, if you don't mind."

Mr. Skillington scratched his chin, something Cole was also predisposed to do. "Actually, I do mind. Not only am I pleased with your work, Anna, but that would leave me without anyone to head up my marketing department."

"Cole can easily step into the job."

He crossed his arms over his chest. "True, but Cole resigned less than an hour ago."

Anna swallowed, shook her head. "But he can't have. He's your son. Skillington Ski is his future."

"Nevertheless, he said he can no longer work for Skillington in any capacity."

"But..." Anna tried to make sense of it but couldn't. She needed Cole to explain why he'd done such a thing. She looked wildly about the room but couldn't locate him. "Where is he?"

"Gone," Mr. Skillington said.

Anna retreated from him, then took another step before spinning on her heel and rushing toward the door.

"Anna, where are you going?" he called after her. "We're not through talking. I didn't tell you where—"

The rest of his words were lost to her as she wrenched open the door and stepped past the threshold. Cole was gone, driven away by her intractability, by her refusal to trust him. How could she ever make things right with him?

She walked down the steps with her head bowed, her hands shoved into her pockets, her heart hurting. When she heard soft footfalls coming up the sidewalk, she lifted her head, intending to let the new arrival pass.

She noticed the long, black, familiar overcoat first. Her heart hammered while her eyes traveled upward over the man's tall frame to his strong, even features and the professor glasses that seemed so contradictory in relation to the very virile package he presented.

Cole.

Her feet froze in place while she blinked a few times to make sure he wasn't a mirage. But still he stood there, solid, strong and oh, so very sexy.

"What are you doing here?" she managed to ask.

"Looking for you," he answered.

She barely processed his answer. "Your father said you were gone. I thought he meant gone for good, but here you are...." She angled her head. "What do you mean you're looking for me?"

"I went to your parents' house but Julie told me you were here." His hands were in his pockets and he seemed to be holding his shoulders stiffly. He sounded more unsure of himself than she'd ever heard him when he asked, "Why did you come here?"

She bit her lip. "To resign."

He released a short, audible breath. His head shook

back and forth. "But that makes no sense," he protested. "You love that job."

It was time to take that leap of faith, Anna thought.

"Not half as much as I love you," she said softly. Her lips trembled, but it had nothing to do with the cold. "Oh, Cole, can you forgive me?"

In answer, he opened his arms. She walked into them, knowing that's where she'd belonged all along, and their mouths met in a hungry kiss. Any doubts she'd had disappeared in the power of their embrace. He'd put a claim on her heart days ago. It was time she willingly gave it to him.

The door to Mr. Skillington's home must have been partially open, because she heard voices raised in unison counting down from ten. She and Cole didn't break off their kiss until the party guests proclaimed the entrance of the new year with noisemakers and horns.

She watched from Cole's arms while the sky filled with a brilliant array of red, gold and green fireworks somebody had set off in the distance.

"That's what it feels like inside when you kiss me," Anna said, reaching up to stroke his cheek. "But I was afraid of that feeling. I made everything about the job because I was afraid to trust you."

"I quit the job," he said, smoothing her hair back from her face. "I never want you to think that a job is more important to me than you are."

"I know that now," she said, "but I don't think your father should accept your resignation either."

"He didn't accept yours?" One corner of his mouth kicked up. "Smart man, my father. I'm lucky to have him. But I'm not so sure he needs both of us to market his ski equipment."

"He doesn't. He needs me to market ski equipment and you to promote the new cycling department I'm going to suggest he start." She smiled at the idea that had been brewing in her mind. "Think about it, Cole. What if there is no problem with how Skillington is being run? What if diversification is the answer to increasing profits?"

"You mean Skillington should sell bikes to keep it afloat in the summer months?" he asked.

She nodded eagerly. "If your father goes for it, you'd be a tremendous asset. You know bikes, Cole. And you dislike winter sports and the cold, anyway."

"I don't know about that." Cole gazed up at the sky as it begin to fill with fat white flakes and then back down at her. "Since I met you, winter's grown on me. It's the season I fell in love."

"I know what you mean," she said, secure and happy in his arms. "I've always loved Christmas, but never as much as this year. I didn't get a potbellied pig, but this year, I did get Co—"

He put gloved fingers against her mouth to interrupt her. Laughter filled his eyes. "I sense you're going to say something corny. Don't you want to wait until your grandfather's around to hear it?"

"Haven't you paid any attention to my family at all?" she answered, shaking her head in mock consternation. "They already know I got Cole for Christmas."

HARLEQUIN®

Temptation®

Coming to a bookstore near you...

**The True Blue Calhouns trilogy
by bestselling author Julie Kistler**

Meet Jake, a cop who plays by the rules in

#957 HOT PROSPECT
(January 2004)

Deal with Sean, rebel and police detective in

#961 CUT TO THE CHASE
(February 2004)

Fall for Coop, rookie with a yen for danger in

#965 PACKING HEAT
(March 2004)

Three sinfully sexy very arresting men...
Ladies, watch out!

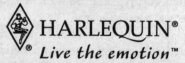

HARLEQUIN®
Live the emotion™

Visit us at www.canwetemptyou.com

HTTBR

HARLEQUIN® Blaze™

In L.A., nothing remains confidential for long...

KISS & TELL

Don't miss

Tori Carrington's

exciting new miniseries featuring four
twentysomething friends—
and the secrets they *don't* keep.

Look for:

#105—NIGHT FEVER
October 2003

#109—FLAVOR OF THE MONTH
November 2003

#113—JUST BETWEEN US...
December 2003

Available wherever Harlequin books are sold.

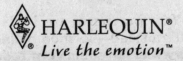

HARLEQUIN®
Live the emotion™

Visit us at www.eHarlequin.com   HBKNT

eHARLEQUIN.com

Looking for today's most popular
books at great prices?
At www.eHarlequin.com, we offer:

- An **extensive selection** of romance
  books by top authors!

- **New** releases, Themed Collections
  and hard-to-find **backlist.**

- A sneak peek at Upcoming books.

- Enticing book **excerpts** and **back
  cover copy!**

- Read recommendations from other
  readers (and post your own)!

- Find out what everybody's reading
  in **Bestsellers.**

- **Save BIG** with everyday discounts
  and exclusive online offers!

- Easy, convenient **24-hour shopping.**

- Our **Romance Legend** will help select
  reading that's *exactly* right for you!

**Your purchases are 100%
guaranteed—so shop online
at www.eHarlequin.com today!**

INTBB1

eHARLEQUIN.com

Your favorite authors are just a click away
at www.eHarlequin.com!

- Take our **Sister Author Quiz** and
  we'll match you up with the author
  most like you!

- Choose from over 500
  author **profiles!**

- Chat with your favorite authors
  on our **message boards.**

- Are you an author in the making?
  Get advice from published authors
  in **The Inside Scoop!**

- Get the latest on **author appearances**
  and tours!

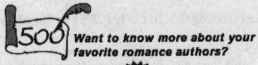

500 *Want to know more about your
favorite romance authors?*

Choose from over 500 author profiles!

**Learn about your favorite authors
in a fun, interactive setting—
visit www.eHarlequin.com today!**

INTAUTH

**If you're a fan of sensual romance
you *simply* must read...**

The third sizzling title in Carly Phillips's *Simply* trilogy.

"4 STARS—Sizzle the winter blues away with a *Simply Sensual*
tale...wonderful, alluring and fascinating!"
—*Romantic Times*

Available in January 2004.

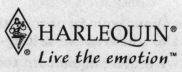

Visit us at www.eHarlequin.com

PHSSCP3

Stories of shocking truths revealed!

PRIVATE SCANDALS

A brand-new collection from

JOANNA WAYNE
JUDY CHRISTENBERRY
TORI CARRINGTON

From three of the romance genre's most enthralling authors
comes this trio of novellas about secret agendas, deep passions
and hidden pasts. But not all scandals can be kept private!

Coming in January 2004.

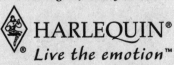

HARLEQUIN®
Live the emotion™

Visit us at www.eHarlequin.com

PHPS

HARLEQUIN
Temptation

THE WRONG BED

What happens when a girl finds herself in the *wrong* bed...with the *right* guy?

Find out in:

#866 NAUGHTY BY NATURE by Jule McBride
February 2002

#870 SOMETHING WILD by Toni Blake
March 2002

#874 CARRIED AWAY by Donna Kauffman
April 2002

#878 HER PERFECT STRANGER by Jill Shalvis
May 2002

#882 BARELY MISTAKEN by Jennifer LaBrecque
June 2002

#886 TWO TO TANGLE by Leslie Kelly
July 2002

Midnight mix-ups have never been so much fun!

HARLEQUIN®
Makes any time special ®

Visit us at www.eHarlequin.com

HTNBN2